Chapter One

The relative tranquillity of a drunken slur coating the files and documents on the desk was shattered by a layer of golden-brown whiskey. The room had not enjoyed fresh air for months; the once rich mahogany scent in the study now replaced by a combination of stale alcohol and tobacco. Photographs containing former glories looked down upon Charles as he clumsily attempted to clean up his spillage, still not quite aware of what is going on after this rude awakening. He frantically dabbed the folders with a cloth but the whiskey still seeped through, staining every page to highlight the plight each has suffered.

A series of framed newspaper clippings seem determined to convince the world of the greatness of Charles Ainsworth but are at odds with the forlorn figure below. A number of University degrees also cast damning judgement upon him. Charles' hands shake violently as he casts aside the first cloth, dripping with the dregs of whiskey that it managed to rescue from the desk. He gathered a second cloth but not realising it was dirty, he spread remnants of ash and dirt over the desk, forming a putrid mixture as it combined with the whiskey.

Disposing of the subservient cloth Charles rises from his desk to search for anything that might stop the liquid spreading. His eyes struggle to adjust to the bright daylight which is now creeping into the study. He scans the room looking for anything that might help him. A quick glance back to his desk revealed that the whiskey was now running freely upon the surface. Charles darts back to try and save the files, throwing them onto the floor in a desperate attempt to limit the casualties of this attack. Again he looks around the room and his eyes are drawn to a yellow pillow perched proudly upon a leather settee. If Charles cast his mind back this pillow might have reminded him of happier times but his current state of panic, mixed with the alcohol in his system, mean that reminiscing is unlikely. He snatches the pillow from the settee and sprints awkwardly to the desk. However, in his haste he forgot about the files on the floor and Charles' balance is non-existent as he trips over the pile of documents, smashing his head off the corner of his desk on his way to the floor.

Charles lays motionless on the hard wooden floor. Droplets of whiskey plummet from the desktop like Chinese water torture; each landing upon his statuesque frame to celebrate the victory of their emancipation.

*****

Robert had risen early. He knew how important this day was and felt determined to give it his full attention. A clean-shaven, sharp looking individual looked back at him as he adjusted his tie in the bathroom mirror. His dark hair was still damp from the shower and he ran a comb through it, styling his dark locks in the fashion he always employed when he was going to be appearing in court. The finishing touches to his wardrobe were being applied when he heard a loud thud from his father's study. Robert turned immediately and hurried along the corridor, breaking into a sprint as he made his way to the grand staircase at the end of the landing. He hurdled down the stairs three at a time and burst into his father's study. The stench of whiskey filled his nostrils as he entered but he could not see his father. Robert opened the curtains, allowing the morning light which had thus far been forbidden to burst into the study without fear of trespass. It was then he noticed a puddle of liquid on the desk and as his eyes followed this he noticed his father's legs protruding from the other end of the desk. Robert's heart immediately began to beat at a faster pace as he rushed over.

Charles was unconscious but Robert was relieved to see he was still breathing. He sat his father up and gently shook him. Charles' head fell to one side, revealing a deep cut just above his right temple. Robert shook Charles slightly harder and this produced a small reaction as his father let out a sorrowful groan. Robert laid him back down and looked at the pile of damp and disorganised files that lay scattered at his feet. Immediately his heart sank as he knew that today's task had just become much more difficult. Charles let out another groan, this time a touch louder and began to rub his head as he regained consciousness. Robert got up and made his way to the chair at the top of the desk. Settling down into the rich, leather comfort he placed his head in his hands and asked God for strength. His silent reflection was disturbed by another moan from Charles, who was beginning to move more freely, though still not yet rising to his feet. Robert opened the top drawer of the desk to reveal another bottle of whiskey, along with a picture of someone very familiar.

"Oooh, my head is killing me. What happened Robert?"

'I don't think it's your head that's killing you', thought Robert as he pushed the drawer shut.

"Anyway, shake it off – you're fine. We have to be in court in an hour."

Robert knew that appearing in court would be the last thing on his father's mind but it was particularly important that he attended today.

"I don't think I'll make it Robert, my head's really sore. I think I could've done some damage. Sure you'll be fine without me."

"Listen, you're head is fine and you have to come today. Mr Aldridge has been asking for you and I can't keep making excuses. Now please, go upstairs and clean yourself up. I'll make my way to court now to meet with him but I'll be informing our client that you will be along shortly."

With that Robert left the study. He knew that Charles did not want to go but he decided, or rather hoped his father's conscience would eventually ensure his appearance. By leaving he also knew he was denying his father the opportunity to plead with him any further.

Robert readjusted his tie in the mirror and once again ran a comb through his hair, hoping that his cool outward appearance would conceal the fear and nervousness that was growing inside him. He took a deep breath and checked himself one last time in the hallway mirror before stepping out into the crisp morning air.

Robert's breath was visible as he quickly paced the driveway towards the Kennelworth road. The stones underfoot were packed tightly together as the morning ground frost had not yet thawed.

He had arranged to meet Mr Aldridge outside the courthouse and needed to be there in good time, especially as he was still unsure if his father would be attending. This was a road that Charles had travelled many times but had very rarely walked. However, since the car had been deemed an unnecessary, or more accurately an unaffordable expense, Robert was left with little choice but to make the two-mile journey by foot.

As he began the incline that led to the courthouse, Robert anxiously checked his wrist watch. He had hoped to arrive early to review the details once again in his head however, and in keeping with his morning thus far, as he rounded the corner there stood the short, squat figure of Mr Aldridge.

"Good morning sir."

"Let's hope so", replied Mr Aldridge abruptly.

"And where is your father?"

Robert could tell by Mr Aldridge's tone that he was not impressed.

"He's just running over the final details again in his study. I'm quite sure he will be joining us shortly."

"Well he better. When I hired Mr Ainsworth QC I didn't expect to be getting his son."

"Like I said sir, he'll be joining us shortly. Shall we go inside?"

With that the two figures pushed open the doors and entered the grand stone building.

******

With all his being Charles craved the comfort and safety of his bed. The thought of entering a courtroom made him feel physically sick but his conscience would not allow him to abandon Robert. The guilt was gnawing inside him, just like the pain was doing to his head.

He gingerly climbed upstairs and made his way to the bathroom. It was a pair of heavy, blood-shot eyes that confronted him in the mirror as he splashed cold water over his face. He knew he should shave but time was against him. Instead he washed his face and styled his hair as best he could. He then changed into his court attire, a fine silk gown and buttoned jacket but could not find his wig. Undeterred, he continued to ready himself, confident that his wig would be in the study.

Despite his uncomfortable start to the morning, Charles looked remarkably fresh as he studied himself in the mirror. The cut he sustained to his head was almost completely disguised by the way he had combed his hair. In fact, if his hands were not shaking he would have given the impression of a man completely balanced in both mind and body.

He quickly marched across the landing and down the stairs to his study. He gathered the files that had caused so much strife this morning and forced them into his briefcase. He then searched the room for his wig. After a quick glance of his watch he began to look more frantically, throwing aside books and documents that interfered with his search. He then sat down in his chair and looked across the top of his desk. Some pages and files soaked in whiskey still laid there but there was no sign of the wig. Charles then, without thought, opened the top drawer of his desk and immediately froze.

A pair of dark hazel eyes stared back at him. They seemed so alive and intense, yet sympathetic and full of understanding. Charles lifted the photo and stared at it as the sensation of hundreds of daggers simultaneously pierced his heart. A tear fell and landed on the photo, spreading out across the glass frame and blurring the identities of both people in the picture. Charles wiped the photo and continued to look longingly at the attractive woman who stood alongside him. His hands began to quiver as painful memories came flooding back. He could remember every detail of the day the photo was taken; the warm sunshine on the back of his neck, the gently breeze which playfully tossed his wife's long dark hair, the smell of the ocean and the sound of waves crashing upon the shore. Charles had revisited this place every night in his dreams for the past three years and every morning his heart broke once again as he woke up to find himself alone.

His painful reminiscing was interrupted by the ticking of the clock, which seemed louder than before, as if deliberately seeking to capture Charles' attention. But now there could be no disguising that Charles was not in control of his emotions and, as had become common practise recently, he reached for some comfort. He lifted the lid off the whiskey bottle that also resided in the drawer and put the bottle to his lips. The peaty aroma made Charles gag as he took a large mouthful. His lips were burning but Charles was not satisfied. He returned the photo to the top drawer and closed it. He then reached down and opened the third drawer down to reveal a silver hip flask. This had originally been a present, meant as a decorative piece only, but had been employed on a regular basis recently. He grabbed the flask and carried it to the drinks cabinet in the corner of the study. His hands were unsteady as he poured, resulting in some whiskey over-flowing as he topped up the flask. He then sealed the lid and placed the flask inside his chest pocket.

Aware that he was running very late Charles turned to leave but his left foot nudged something obstructing his path. He turned round to find his barrister's wig sat proudly upon his foot stool, perfectly unaware of the damage it had caused him. Charles would have to hurry.

******

Robert led Mr Aldridge into the foyer of the courthouse, where a well-dressed concierge greeted them.
"Can I help you gentlemen?"
"We are waiting for Mr Ainsworth", said Mr Aldridge in a dismissive fashion.
"No we're fine thanks Edwin. We'll just make our way up to one of the offices if that's alright?"
"No problem Robert, room 7A is free. If you need anything please give me a bell."
"Thank you Edwin. When my father arrives can you please inform him that we are there?"
"Of course."

Edwin gave Robert a friendly wink, then turned and walked back to the front desk. Robert escorted the increasingly agitated Mr Aldridge along the hallway and held open the door into room 7A. Mr Aldridge was constantly checking his watch and seemed to be growing angrier with every second that passed without Charles being in attendance.

"Let's just go over the details one last time Mr Aldridge," said Robert, eager to appease his growing temper.

Mr Aldridge had good reason to be anxious. Rumours of his underhanded business activities had been circulating for years, although it was only now that a case had finally been brought against him. Robert knew this was going to be a difficult case and that he and Charles would have to work very hard to convince a jury of Mr Aldridge's innocence. What was more disconcerting for Robert was that Mr Aldridge had hired Charles purely upon his reputation – or more accurately, his former reputation. Mr Aldridge would have read in the newspapers over the years that Charles was a great barrister, but the man who would be joining them - or at least Robert hoped would be joining them - was unrecognisable from the dynamic figure of previous years.

As Robert sorted through a number of documents and banking transactions with Mr Aldridge he became increasingly nervous. The clock was showing 11.05am and there was still no sign of Charles. Then there was a loud knock on the door. Robert breathed a sigh of relief but it was Edwin who stepped into the room.

"Sorry to disturb you gentlemen. Robert may I have a word?"

"Of course. Please excuse me."

As he stepped out of the room Robert knew from the look on Edwin's face that this was not good news.

"What is it Edwin?"

"I'm afraid it's your father."

"What about him?"

"Well, he has arrived but I don't think he is in a fit state."

"Where is he?"

"I escorted him to the bathroom and told him to freshen up. Ordinarily I would've sent him home Robert but I know the situation you're in. I should warn you though that Lord Stephens does not take kindly to people appearing in his court who are under the influence of alcohol. You'd better pull him together, and quickly."

"Thanks Edwin. Can you please tell Mr Aldridge that I have been summoned for a quick debriefing by Lord Stephens and will be back shortly?"

"Of course Robert, good luck."

With that Robert turned and sprinted down the marble corridor towards the gents' bathroom, his every stride echoing loudly around the old building. He burst into the bathroom and was shocked to discover that his father was not alone.

"Good morning Robert. What brings you here?" said a man supporting the limp frame of Charles as he wretched over the toilet.

The figure supporting was Hector, an old friend of Charles' who Robert had met on a number of occasions and was not sure whether he liked him or not. At this particular moment however Robert was not in the mood for pleasantries.

"Take one fucking guess Hector. How long have you been here?"

"I was coming into the building and saw Edwin direct him towards the bathroom. What time are you due in court?"

"We start at midday although Mr Aldridge wants to see him now."

"I'll bet he does that crooked bastard. Robert I can stay with Charles here and try and sober him up a bit. You go and keep Mr Aldridge happy. Oh, by the way, what judge is presiding?"

"Lord Stephens."

"Lord Stephens! Bloody hell, Charles can certainly pick his moments! Good luck son, I'll do everything I can to sort him out."

"Thanks Hector, I'll call down before we go into court."

Robert left the bathroom in dire straits but was sure of one thing, he liked Hector.

****

Charles stomach ached as he wretched again over the toilet. There seemed to be nothing left but every dry heave was straining his abdominal muscles, causing him immense pain. Sweat was running off his forehead and his eyed were watering. Hector insisted that Charles keep trying to vomit to make absolutely sure there was no alcohol remaining.

"I'm fine Hector, give me peace for one minute" said Charles, his words slurring out the side of his mouth in a clumsy fashion.

"Charles, just relax and take deep breaths. We'll be out of here shortly. I just want to talk to you about this case."

"What case?" asked Charles, his eyes dancing about in a desperate attempt to focus upon Hector.

"The Aldridge case you daft bugger. Do you know what you have to do; are you familiar with the details?"

"Oh yes sir………thank you sir. What fucking difference does it make? You know and I know that that bastard is guilty, might as well let the jury know!"

"Charles! Get a grip of yourself!"

Hector grabbed Charles and forcibly pushed him up against the wall.

"Now you may not think that this case matters a damn, but you are not just hurting yourself, you're bringing Robert down with you. How do you think it'll affect his reputation if you go in there and make a fool of yourself? Think about your son for God's sake!"

"Don't tell me how to look after my son!"

Hector continued, undeterred by Charles' aggressive demeanour.

"Look, I know I haven't been through what you've been through. But we go back a long way and its killing me to see you like this. Sarah has gone and as hard as… Smash!

A crushing blow to the head from Charles spectacularly interrupted Hector. His legs wobbled under the force of the punch and he dropped to the bathroom floor.

"Don't you ever mention her name! Do you hear me? Don't you ever mention her name!"

Charles was fuming as he stormed out of the room and marched forcefully up the corridor towards room 7A, leaving Hector in a bloodied mess in the bathroom.

****

Robert had just completed the final de-brief when the door burst open. He was shocked to see his father and jumped up immediately to try and pre-empt a potentially explosive situation.

"Mr Aldridge, I'd like to introduce you to my father Charles Ainsworth", stuttered Robert.

"Well, I'm delighted to finally meet you. You have quite the reputation, although I was not aware that you were such a difficult man to get the hold off. Perhaps now you can finally give my case the proper attention, rather than having your assistant do the work."

Robert was agitated by Mr Aldridge's comment but would happily ignore it if Charles was capable of putting on a good performance.

"Well Mr Aldridge, I'm sorry to have proved so elusive. I thought that a man of your business sense would have been able to track me down, whether by hook or by crook."

Robert stepped in to relieve the tension.

"Well gents, I believe it is time to enter the court. Mr Aldridge I'd like a quick word with my father. Would you be so kind as to wait for us at the entrance to the courtroom?"

"I suppose I shall have to, won't I? Make sure and be quick, I am paying for your time after all."

Robert held the door open to allow Mr Aldridge to exit, closing it sharply behind him to ensure his father did not leave the room.

"How much have you had to drink?"

"What are you talking about Robert? I haven't had a drop now get out of my way"

Robert was in no mood to be toyed with but his father continued to plead his innocence, arguing vehemently as if trying to also convince himself that he was telling the truth.

"Right, we'll go in now but please remember how important this is. I'll be keeping a close eye on you."

"Listen son, I think I know by now how to handle myself in the courtroom. Perhaps I should be the one to keep an eye on you," quipped Charles, arrogantly.

"Very well, you do that. Now let's go."

Robert turned and pulled open the old wooden door for his father. As the two men marched towards the courtroom, the sense of occasion started to dawn upon Robert and he said a silent prayer – could he successfully represent his client, could his father successfully defend him and, most worryingly, could his father keep it together?

Chapter Two

"I'm afraid it's bad news."

The words Charles had been dreading had finally been delivered. This moment had haunted his dreams for months but still he wasn't prepared. How could anyone be prepared?

"How long?"

"I can't give you an accurate assessment, however there are some....."

"How long!"

"I know this is difficult but please, try and remain calm."

Charles swallowed hard;

"I'm sorry. In your opinion, how long are we talking about?"

The sentence hung in the air for a few seconds as the doctor removed his glasses and breathed heavily on them. He then carefully removed a small cloth from his case and cleaned each lens. Charles sensed he was considering how best to deliver the bad news.

"It's very aggressive. Even with treatment there is not much that can prevent the growth at this stage."

"Please, just tell me how long she has."

"Three months at most. I am so sorry."

The pain was etched upon the doctor's face; years of delivering such sad news having taken its toll.

"If you'd like I can take you in to see her now. Or if you'd prefer a few moments I can step out."

Charles inhaled deeply. He knew he had to face this nightmare and that now was the time to do so.

"Its fine, I'll see her now please."

****

Time stood still as Robert paced up and down the station. The clock overhead suggested that the train should have arrived but as he nervously walked back and forth there was no sign of it. Only a few years ago Robert had been in a rush to leave home; now he was being punished for this by having his return delayed.

    His father had not said much when they spoke, just that his mother was ill and that he should come immediately. Robert had wanted to ask questions but this was the first they'd spoken for a long time and he sensed Charles was in no mood for conversation. The venom of their last words spoken in anger still hung over the pair like a dark cloud. Robert began to cast his mind back but his thoughts were shattered by the loud blast of a horn. The large black train came into view, preceded by a cloud of thick dark smoke. Its steady rhythmic beat descended to a calmer pace and then came the piercing screech of brakes as the train came to a stop.

      Robert stepped on and entered the first carriage. It contained only three travellers; a man in his forties reading a broadsheet newspaper and an elderly couple sitting side by side. Robert nodded to the pair as he walked past and sat down by the window. After a few moments the train's heartbeat was revived once again and as it began to gain momentum and cascade through the countryside Robert could feel his heartbeat increasing too. He had always dreaded returning home and now he was doing so to say goodbye to the person who had made his stay there tolerable.

******

The woman who lay on the bed was unrecognisable from the person Charles had built a life with. She looked tired; her body ravaged by the cancer that grew inside her. Charles sensed recognition in her weary eyes as she opened them and he gave her a warm smile. She tried to smile back but her skin was tight and her expression turned to a grimace. Charles placed his hand on hers to comfort her. He had vowed not to cry but seeing her in such discomfort was more painful than anything he'd ever experienced. He swallowed hard and cleared his throat.
"Darling, I've......I've spoken with the doctor."
Charles could feel tears welling up. He turned his gaze to the floor and clenched his fist hard to try and stop them.
"It's not good news I'm afraid pet. I......I don't quite know how to tell you this..."
Tears began rolling down his face, like emigrants crossing a foreign border.
"The doctor says............he says that you don't have long. But I know you're a fighter........"
Charles was squeezing her hand as hard as he could, if only he could pass his strength to her. He wiped his eyes and continued.
"We'll get you the best medical attention possible."
Charles held her gaze for what seemed an eternity. He knew she had comprehended his words but through his tear-filled eyes he hadn't detected any

reaction. Inside he knew that whatever fight she had left would not be enough; her body had already surrendered.

****

The sound of hurried footsteps reverberated around the marble corridor as Robert made his way to the Intensive Care Unit. A smell of detergent filled his nostrils and he didn't know if it was this, or something deeper, that was making him gag. He took a second to compose himself, taking a series of deep breaths in and out through his mouth before starting out again towards the ward.

It wasn't until Robert looked through the door's window pane that the gravity of the situation fully dawned on him. His mother, who had always been so full of life, now lay frail and helpless upon the bed. She had aged considerably since he had seen her last. A series of tubes, wires and the constant beeping of a heart monitor were the only signs that she was still part of this world. Sat next to her was a man Robert hadn't spoken to in years. He also looked much older, with deep set wrinkles in his forehead. Robert stood motionless, transfixed by the sight until he saw his father wipe a tear from his eye. He had never seen Charles weep before. This act served to confirm both the futility and finality of the situation – it was a tear of death.

Charles didn't hear the door opening. He sat gazing at his wife and contemplating how cruel a fate had befallen them when his concentration was broken by a gentle cough. He turned to find Robert stood in the centre of the room, his head bowed and his eyes fixed firmly upon his mother. Charles immediately rose to his feet and cast the remnants of a tear away from his cheek.
"Ah Robert, nice of you to finally join us."
Robert said nothing in reply. He was determined not to let his father agitate him; if only for his mother's sake. He stepped over to her bedside and delicately lifted a stray strand of hair away from his mother's brow. She smiled back at him, though Robert could tell it was paining her to do so. She had sorrowful eyes that he sensed saw right through him and into his very soul. Slowly she raised her right hand and beckoned Robert to come closer. He obliged as she removed the mask from her mouth.
"Darling, you shouldn't...."

She raised her hand to silence Charles' protestation and again motioned for Charles to draw nearer. He leant down as she summoned her remaining reserves of strength.

"Robert...........my son..."

Robert knelt down closer; he was struggling to make out her ghostly soft murmurs.

"I'm asking you to do me one final favour."

"Anything," replied Robert, squeezing her hand.

"Make peace with your father."

A wave of emotion swept over him as tears filled his eyes.

"Make peace......and look after each other."

With that she lay back in the bed and her eyes no longer registered with Robert's; they seemed to be looking at something in the distance. Her hand that had been holding the mask suddenly slumped and the heart monitor changed from a regular beep to constant monotone.

"Help, help!" yelled Charles frantically.

A doctor and two nurses burst into the room as Robert still sat by her side. For him it was like being in a dream. He sat there unable to move as time seemed to pass very slowly. Eventually someone ushered him up and a nurse escorted him out of the room, but not before he took one more glance at his mother's eyes. He knew she had already left. She had used her final moments to intertwine his fate with that of his father's and Robert knew there was no escaping that.

Sarah died at 2.07pm, 1960.

Chapter Three

Robert's hands were clammy as he anxiously awaited the arrival of Lord Stevens. He was seated beside Mr Aldridge with Charles on the other side. Mr Aldridge also seemed nervous, commenting on a number of occasions about the judge's lateness, while Charles seemed quite calm by contrast. A substantial crowd was in the gallery, which Robert attributed to the local desire to see Mr Aldridge's crooked business practises eventually coming back to haunt him. However Robert knew that while Mr Aldridge had transgressed, these had been only minor offences. In fact his behaviour had been no more disreputable than a number of other prominent local businessmen who had managed to find themselves cleared of all charges. The great worry in Robert's head was that it would take all his father's skill and experience to convince the jury of Mr Aldridge's relative innocence.

"All rise", bellowed the court clerk, shattering the silence of the courtroom and making Robert's heart unexpectedly skip a flutter.

"Lord Justice Stephens' presiding", continued the clerk as a large stern-looking character positioned himself in the chair before motioning everyone to take their seats.

"In the case of Dylan versus Aldridge, prosecution are you ready to proceed with your opening statement?" asked Lord Stevens, enjoying being the focus of attention. He spoke loudly yet slowly to extend his time in the spotlight.

"We are your honour", replied a bearded barrister who was representing Mr Dylan.

The barrister, Mr Robson, proceeded to explain to the jury exactly what he intended to outline during the course of the trial; that Mr Aldridge had broken an agreed contract with his client regarding the sale of business premises. This, Mr Robson alleged, resulted in substantial financial gain for Mr Aldridge as he subsequently sold the premises to a property developer in a multi-million pound deal. Mr Robson also alleged that Mr Aldridge had offered financial incentives to members of the local council to grant planning permission to the developer for areas surrounding his premises, thereby increasing the value of his property. In total Mr Robson had painted quite an ugly picture of the business practises of Mr Aldridge, which seemed to find favour with the onlookers in the gallery.

Throughout the barrister's opening statement, Robert fixed his gaze upon his father. His heart sank as he noticed Charles' head nodding back and forth as if trying not to surrender to sleep. On one awkward occasion Mr Aldridge spotted this rocking motion, at which point Robert poured a glass of water and set it loudly in front of

Charles to startle him out of this trance. This had the desired effect as Charles jolted back into full consciousness, only to see Mr Aldridge casting him an angry glare.

As the barrister concluded his speech Charles suddenly felt his hands beginning to tremble. At first only a slight twitch but, as Lord Stevens encouraged Charles to make his opening statement, his hands were shaking uncontrollably. His pulse was also racing. The thought crossed his mind that he might be having a heart attack. Charles longed for death to take him so that he would no longer feel this great pain but this wish was not granted.

Robert noticed his father's hands trembling as he tried to lift a folder from his briefcase. He also saw the beads of sweat appearing on his father's brow and knew that he couldn't go on.

"If it pleases the court I would ask for a five minute recess as I have an urgent matter to discuss with my client's barrister", said Robert.

The judge was visibly not impressed by the request but, with a theatrical roll of his eyes, he granted Robert's wish.

Robert rose to his feet to approach his father but before he got to him Charles was off striding down the centre of the courtroom and out through the large wooden doors. Robert followed, conscious that he didn't want to be seen as running after his father. He too burst through the wooden doors but Charles was nowhere in sight. Robert broke into full stride as he raced down the corridor, searching frantically in every room he passed to see if he could find Charles, but to no avail. He ran as far as the entrance, hoping that Edwin might be of some help.

"Have you seen my father Edwin?"

"Not since this morning. He hasn't come this direction; is there anything I can help you with?"

Robert turned sharply and jogged back up the corridor, offering a disgruntled 'no' as he did so.

Robert was left with no other option; he would have to apologise to the judge and excuse both him and Charles from the case. That would undoubtedly result in Mr Aldridge dropping them but Robert could not find any possible solution. He waited outside the courtroom for a few moments, gathering his breath while praying his father would appear. His prayers were not answered however as his father did not materialise. Therefore with a deep breath he opened the large door and stepped into the courtroom, only to be greeted by a most curious sight.

****

When the judge granted Robert's request for a five minute recess, Charles felt an overwhelming sense of relief. Albeit this was a temporary reprieve but Charles knew he had been given an opportunity which he had to take. He also knew Robert would want to talk with him so he immediately headed for the door. Charles could hear increasingly loud footsteps behind him which he presumed to be Robert as he marched down the courtroom, so upon exiting he dashed round the corner and towards a nearby set of stairs.

Under the staircase, almost invisible to the eye, lay a small door which Charles and a few fellow barristers had discovered some years ago. The door was to allow staff quicker access from the kitchen to the dining room as a corridor connected the two. The corridor also contained a number of small reading rooms which provided a safe haven for Charles and a few colleagues to enjoy the occasional game of poker alongside a Cuban cigar or glass of brandy. Once again if Charles was afforded the luxury of reminiscing he might reflect on some happy times but he was unable to do so. He forced the hesitant door open and squeezed in, just as he heard the courtroom doors opening.

Charles heard the patter of loud footsteps running up and down the marble corridor outside but he did not care. Instead he made his way into one of the reading rooms. He came upon a door slightly ajar and peered inside to see if it was empty. It was indeed empty but the room also appeared colder and somehow smaller than Charles remembered as he entered the room. It was dark, with only a small slither of light creeping between the curtains to provide some illumination. Charles sensed that the room had not welcomed a visitor for quite some time, the only evidence that people had spent any time there being a faint scent of cigar smoke which still hung in the air.

Charles settled himself into one of the large leather seats and for a second he actually felt relaxed, as if the chair was momentarily guarding him. However, as his eyes panned the room the unfortunate circumstances he was facing slowly crept back into his mind. He looked down at his still shaking hands and, without a further moment's thought, reached for his silver hip flask. Once again the whiskey burned his lips as he dribbled some onto his chin. It felt warm as the alcohol hit the back of his throat. He took another mouthful from the flask and began to think about staying hidden there until the evening. Would that be such a bad thing? But Robert crept into his thoughts and, despite the strong temptation, he knew he had to go back. 'If only whiskey could remove my conscience', thought Charles as he rose to his feet and gingerly made his way back towards the courtroom.

****

Robert was astounded to see his father seated at the front of the courtroom beside Mr Aldridge. He marched quickly to their bench but before he got a chance to speak with his father Lord Stephens got proceedings underway once again.

"Order, order I say," bellowed the judge as he hushed the audience in advance of his latest performance.

"Now that the defence has had the opportunity for a small chat, can we please hear an opening statement?"

Lord Stephens fixed his gaze upon Robert as he spoke, emphasizing that he was not happy to have had his time in the limelight cut short.

Charles rose to his feet as he addressed the court,

"We can your honour and I thank you for granting us the courtesy of a brief discussion."

Robert was tense as he watched his father deliver the opening statement. He had drafted the piece and forced Charles to practise it in front of him dozens of times to ensure he knew the key points, but as Charles jumped from one area to the next in a disjointed fashion Robert began to feel physically ill. He slouched in his chair, almost resigned to the fact that the crisis unfolding in front of him could no longer be averted.

Charles' mind was a jigsaw of information that he was clumsily trying to assemble as he spoke. Small nuggets of details would suddenly come to him through a veil of whiskey-clouded thoughts but try as he might Charles was incapable of twisting these together into a coherent argument. As he mumbled sentences comprised of little more than nonsense his heartbeat increased rapidly and his cheeks felt on fire. Charles felt this public act of torture and humiliation would continue indefinitely, until.....

"Good God man........Stop!" howled Mr Aldridge as he rose to his feet.

The gallery rose in anger and began hurling abuse at Mr Aldridge, to which Lord Stephens angrily banged his scabbard twice.

"Your honour, I wish to inform you that this man, this pathetic man, no longer represents me. He is nothing more than a common drunk and I don't want to ever see his useless face again!"

Once again the gallery responded with contempt for Mr Aldridge's outburst.

"Order! Order in court," shouted Lord Stephens as he banged his scabbard frantically in an attempt to silence both Mr Aldridge and those in the gallery.

"There will be order in this courtroom right now or you shall all be paying a most heavy price," snapped the judge as he finally re-established some semblance of control.

"Mr Aldridge and council, get into my private office right now!"

Robert lay motionless in his seat for only a few seconds but it felt like an eternity. He felt frozen as the gravity of what had occurred slowly dawned on him. However, despite the almost overwhelming temptation to let his father face the music on his own, he just couldn't stand the thought of Charles being in there defenceless. Dutifully he rose to his feet and escorted the shell-shocked Charles to the judge's private office at the top end of the courtroom. Mr Aldridge had already made his way there, puffing out his chest and strolling with a swagger in an attempt to infuriate the gallery, a move which had clearly succeeded.

"Shut the door and sit down immediately," barked Lord Stephens.

His swagger suddenly gone, Mr Aldridge scurried towards one of the two chairs facing the judge. Charles gingerly sat on the other while Robert stood at his father's side.

"What is the meaning of all this?" enquired the judge.

"It's his bloody fault," replied Mr Aldridge almost instantaneously. "The man clearly has a drinking problem. I've been made to look a complete fool this morning! I mean to have someone like that represent....."

"Enough, Mr Aldridge." Lord Stephens raised his hand to silence the complaint.

"Charles, have you been drinking today?"

Robert almost whispered the answer he wanted his father to give.

"No your honour, I have not," replied Charles, desperately trying to sound convincing. Robert winced.

The judge rose to his feet in anger. He approached Charles, staring him directly in the eye as he sat down on the edge of the desk next to Charles.

"Your honour if I could."

Robert's intervention was dismissed with a firm wave of the hand as the judge prepared to enjoy another theatrical performance. Charles' heart was pounding and, despite the fact his eyes were fixed firmly upon the floor, he could feel the piercing stare of the judge's eyes upon him. All the years of interrogation and cross examination Lord Stephens had presided over were suddenly coming out as he toyed with his witness.

"Charles, if you have not been drinking then will you not do me the honour of looking me in the eye."

Charles sheepishly raised his head.

"Tell me Charles, is that whiskey I smell on your breath?"

"No sir," muttered Charles.

"Are you sure?"

"Yes quite. I've been suffering with a cold of late and have been on medication so perhaps that is the smell."

Robert rolled his eyes, disgusted by his father's inability to recognise how ridiculous that sounded. He was about to interject once again but before he could Lord Stephens reached into Charles' jacket pocket and removed his silver hip flask.

"What do you take me for? A bloody fool?"

Lord Stephens angrily unscrewed the lid of the flask to be greeted with the strong pungent aroma of whiskey as he held the flask to his nose.

"I told you your honour," sneered Mr Aldridge, vindicated by the judge's elaborate performance.

"Silence! In all my years I have never been treated with such disrespect. I'm well within my rights to hold you in contempt of this court!"

"Please your honour, I beg you", once again Robert was silenced by a wave of the hand.

"As I was saying, before I was so rudely interrupted, I could find you in contempt of court but I fail to see the point in doing so after today's performance. You can rest assured you'll never handle another case in front of any judge in all the land, let alone me."

Lord Stephens turned his attention to Robert,

"And as for you, what kind of representation do you feel you have provided for your client? I can appreciate family loyalty to an extent but when you are soliciting for a client your loyalty should be solely to them, that is why you took that oath when you qualified. The fact that you let your *Barrister* appear in court in such a state shows a complete and utter disregard for the practise of law and that I find completely unforgivable."

Robert felt sick with each punishing word that Lord Stephens delivered, like a boxer on the ropes receiving a volley of hard shots to the body.

"I understand it must be difficult to try and emulate your father's former legal greatness but, as has been clearly demonstrated here today, those days are well and truly over. So now, I suggest you consider another profession. I will be making it my business to inform all those I have dealings with of the incredibly flawed judgement and professionalism of one Robert Ainsworth. Now get out of my sight the pair of you!"

Robert stormed out of the private office, nearly slamming the door in Charles' face as he followed behind and marched angrily down the central aisle of the courtroom. Charles called out for him to slow down but Robert continued apace as he flew down the corridor and out of the courthouse, for the final time.

"Robert, for God's sake slow down."

"Why? So you can stop for another drink!"

A rage was burning inside Robert that was almost beyond control.

"I've never told you this until now but you are fucking pathetic. The fact you're drinking your life away no longer concerns me, but why did you have to bring me down with you?"

With that Robert stormed off. The last thing he wanted to do was spend any time with the person who had just cost both of them their futures.

Chapter Four

Charles' dark, dreamless sleep was cruelly disturbed by a painful, throbbing headache which set in all of a sudden. At first he wasn't familiar with his surroundings but as he came to his senses he slowly began to recognise his living room. Still wearing the same clothes from the day before, he clumsily got up from the settee and made his way towards the bathroom.

He looked weather-beaten and haggard as he stared at his reflection in the mirror. His head was still pounding and his eyes, though not fully open, were heavily bloodshot and glazed over. The inside of his mouth felt stale, with a lingering and sickening taste of alcohol which Charles set about removing as he reached for his toothbrush. The taste of toothpaste and water made Charles gag, signalling opposition to being exposed to something non-alcoholic for the first time in a considerable while. He finished brushing and lifted a handful of cold water to his lips which he felt cool the whole way down into his stomach.

"Robert............Robert, are you here?" Charles' throat was hoarse as he called out around the house in a dishevelled voice.

No reply was forthcoming as he made his way into the kitchen. Above the sink was a cupboard stocked with medicine. Charles reached inside and after lifting three or four different containers, removed two painkillers from the appropriate tub. The pain in his head would soon be sufficiently soothed but until then Charles decided to sit silently at the kitchen table and try to figure out where Robert was. He sat forward and placed his forehead on the table. Within a matter of seconds he was almost asleep when there was an incredibly loud bang at the front door. Charles was suddenly wide awake and dashed over to the drawers beside the sink. Panicking, he lifted a large rolling pin from the second drawer and crept over to his front door, only to be greeted by another violent thump upon the door. This startled Charles and he deserted back a few paces into the hall. Rather than confront the offending person Charles decided to gain a better vantage point. He slowly peaked out from behind a curtain in the hallway to see what fate awaited him on the other side of his door. And there stood his son, swaying as he read from one of the daily papers. Charles put down the rolling pin and opened the front door as Robert read aloud from the paper.

"The clearly intoxicated Mr Ainsworth resembled a figure more at home in the backstreet alehouses and brothels that in the courtroom...."

Robert's eyes were dancing around in his head as he struggled to focus upon his father stood in the doorway.

"Get into the bloody house," urged Charles.

"Wait.....wait...this is my favourite part."

Robert's finger traced down the column on the page,

"A spectacular lack of judgement, from which he will surely never recover....."

Robert looked up at his father.

"From which he will surely never recover."

Robert's voice grew angrier as he repeated the sentence.

"From which he will never recover!"

Charles suddenly had a flashback to what had occurred in court the day before.

"Robert I am so sorry. Please come in and let me explain. I know it's bad but we will be able to sort something out. Just get inside, please."

"There's nothing can be done. You've fucked everything. Even the papers know that we're finished. Did I not explain to you how important this case was? Or perhaps you've secretly been working plenty over the past couple of years, keeping it hidden from me all this time and only pretending to be drinking anything you can get your hands on. Is that what you've been doing, because if so then I'll call Revenue and Customs, the Rates collectors and all the other bastards who are demanding every single penny from us and tell them not to worry, that we've got plenty of money!"

      Charles was left dumb-founded by Robert's remarks but rather than reply he turned on his heels and headed towards the kitchen. This move seemed to have the desired effect as Robert stepped out from the cold morning air and into the house.

"Where have you been?" asked Charles as Robert staggered his way into the kitchen.

"What does it matter?"

"I'll ask once again, where have you been?"

Robert felt his temper beginning to fray.

"Let me get this straight, you make a complete fool of yourself in court and cost us both our jobs and you're going to lecture me about where I've been? Do you have any idea how ridiculous that is?"

"How dare you talk to me like that!" exclaimed Charles, slamming the table with his hand as rose to his feet.

"I'll talk to you whatever way I want!"

 "In this house you will show me some damn respect."

"Respect? I lost all respect for you even before my mother died."

Robert had barely finished his sentence when he was hit with a thunderous punch to the head. This rocked him slightly but as he regained his balance he was met by another punch, this one landing on the bridge of his nose. Robert was enraged and replied with a series of punches but they failed to connect cleanly with his father. He then grabbed Charles and the two men frantically grappled and wrestled each other, smashing plates and glasses as they led a trail of devastation throughout the kitchen. Charles managed to position himself so that he had Robert in a headlock and began squeezing hard upon his throat. Robert was swinging left and right punches into the small of his father's back but they were not sufficiently registering with Charles to force him to release his grip. Robert was beginning to feel light headed and he frantically tried to break free from Charles' grasp. In a desperate last attempt he managed to gather sufficient strength to lift Charles and he held him aloft momentarily. However he lost his balance and both men fell onto and then through the kitchen table, landing in a bloodied mess upon onto the floor.

*****

Hector had not visited the Ainsworth house for some time. As he walked up the drive his mind wandered back to his last visit and the truly harrowing experience that had been. He could vividly remember the look of pain and anguish in Charles' eyes as he arrived for the wake. That day Hector thought Charles looked the very image of a broken man, sadly this had proven to be correct.

A sense of apprehension gripped him as he approached the front door. He was still angry with Charles for attacking him yesterday but he, more than anyone, knew the torment Charles was suffering from. Arriving at the house he was surprised to find the front door open. He stepped inside and knocked the door as he pushed it closed. He proceeded down the hall, calling out with every couple of paces but there was no reply. Then he heard a faint sound of groaning coming from the kitchen. Hector followed it and was shocked to find Charles and Robert both lying on the floor; a half of the now divided kitchen table either side of them. He raced over to Charles and prodded him on the shoulder. Charles responded with a groan.
"I see your father has been giving you some of the treatment he gave me yesterday," said Hector to Robert, who was slowly picked himself up off the floor.
Robert stared at Hector but didn't reply as he staggered his way out of the kitchen. Hector could tell from Robert's expression that he was in no mood for pleasantries or small talk.

With Robert now gone Hector placed his hands under Charles' armpits and hoisted him up onto a chair. Hector then sat down opposite his old friend and was taken aback by just how terrible Charles looked. His once rich head of hair had thinned significantly over the last couple of years, while the wrinkles under his eyes and on his forehead appeared much more deep-set and exaggerated. Charles grimaced with pain as he checked his head for cuts.

"What happened Charles?" asked Hector in as sympathetic a tone as he could muster. This was difficult because he was generally not a sensitive character, besides his head was still sore from Charles' attack yesterday.

"I'm not too sure. Robert's probably just upset because......"

"Because you ended his legal career yesterday," interrupted Hector, not going to allow Charles to harbour any delusions or excuses.

"Listen Charles, you and me go back a long way. It kills me to see what you're doing to yourself. I know I can't understand or appreciate what you've been through; it must be hell. But the thing is, as hard as it sounds, you've got to put these demons behind you."

"It's very easy to say that Hector, it's just not quite that simple when you're the person actually having to go through it."

"That's true but there are people willing to help you. Since Sarah's passing you've cut everyone out of your life. Now I don't hold any grudges about you attacking me yesterday but that was you cutting me out again when all I wanted to do was help."

The mention of his late wife's name once again served to inflame Charles' anger.

"Oh all you wanted to do was help? More likely you wanted me off the case so that you could step in and steal my thunder. You've always been jealous of me, haven't you?"

"Shut up you damn fool! Of course I didn't want your case. I'm not interested in making headlines, I'm glad to see you still are though!"

Hector pointed at the paper that Robert had been reading.

"That's why you were with me in the bathroom; you were trying to convince me to go home so that the case would be yours. It all makes sense," continued Charles.

"Get a grip Charles! I'm not going to sit here and listen to this nonsense!"

With that Hector got up and walked to the kitchen door. As he placed his hand on the door he looked back to see Charles still in his seat, motionless as he stared out the window.

"Look Charles, I wanted to come by here to try and help. If you don't want my help that's fine, but sooner or later the realisation will hit you that you cannot work as a legal practitioner here anymore."

Hector reached into his chest pocket and removed a letter which he placed upon the counter.

"I thought this might be of interest. Please consider it as a serious option.......and remember Charles, it's not just you who can't work here anymore."

Chapter Five

As Charles poured himself another large glass of whiskey he tried to remember why he had started drinking today in the first place. It felt cold as he walked into the kitchen, where the table had still not been replaced following his scuffle with Robert a few days previously. Charles set his glass down on the counter and once again read over the details of the letter Hector had left him. He took a large sip and grimaced as the whiskey burned his throat. His eyes were struggling to focus on the text as he attempted to scroll down the letter.

"This is nonsense," he slurred.

"Bloody........eh, rubbish," he continued, opining on the subject matter of the letter to a non-existent audience.

With a final disgruntled remark he crushed the letter in his hand and threw it towards the bin; the letter missing the target and coming to rest beside one of the broken halves of the table. Charles' eyes felt heavy as he lifted the glass and took another mouthful. His stomach was aching with hunger but he knew there was no food in the house. For a brief second he contemplated heading to the local shop but that would mean walking over a quarter of a mile in the bitter cold so he opted against it. Charles would wait for Robert's arrival, confident he would pick up enough sustenance for the pair of them. One final mouthful finished off the remnants of the whiskey. With that Charles decided to rest and so made his way over to a settee in the living room. As had so often been the case recently he fell asleep the instance his head hit the pillow; his conscience taken hostage by another dark and dreamless sleep.

*****

Robert's palms were sweaty as he sat at the desk of Mr Telford. This was a worrying omen as he remembered vividly what occurred the last time he noticed his hands perspiring. He had arrived dressed in his finest suit and once again styled his hair in his preferred fashion but inside he was nervous. He lifted and drank from the cup of coffee that the assistant had provided and tried to calm down by taking a few deep breaths. But just as he finished a large inhalation the door opened and in walked Mr Telford.

"Sorry to have kept you waiting Robert."

"No problem at all," replied Robert, rising to his feet to shake Mr Telford's outstretched hand. On the way round to his seat Mr Telford stopped at the window and opened the blinds, allowing the morning sunshine to filter into the room.

"It's bright this morning," he said cheerily.

"Yes indeed, bright but cold."

Mr Telford sat down opposite Robert. He removed his glasses and wiped them with a cloth before re-applying them to his face. As the morning sunshine reflected off his bald scalp he looked every inch the archetypal bank manager.

"Now Robert, what can I do for you?"

"Well Mr Telford, I'm afraid we're going to need some more time to meet our current loan repayment arrangements."

"Is that so," he replied, leaning back in his chair, "that is disappointing."

"I assure you sir, we will have the money soon, it's just there has been a small complication recently but we will have this sorted as soon as possible."

"Robert tell me, would this complication be due to the fact that you and your father are both currently unemployed and, more seriously, without any prospect of future employment for the foreseeable future?"

"I see you're well informed," said Robert dejectedly.

"Robert, this is where my job becomes painful. I'm afraid I cannot, in all good conscience, permit another extension on your loan. A key factor in allowing such a request would be the consideration of your future employment opportunities but, as I understand it, there are none."

Robert's pulse was racing as Mr Telford continued;

"I'm very sorry but if you do not have your next repayment then the bank will be forced to take ownership of your house."

"But Mr Telford if you could only."

"I'm sorry Robert but there's really nothing I can do. The rules of the loan agreement are very clear, besides I've already given you one extension, I can't give another one otherwise I wouldn't be doing my job properly."

Robert thought about pleading once more but knew in his heart that this would be a fruitless effort. Instead he silently rose to his feet and walked out of the office, leaving the door ajar as he left. Once again he had been dealt a savage blow and did not know where to turn. He walked out the front door of the bank and headed home, trying to figure out how he was going to break the news to his father that they were about to lose the family home.

*****

A wave of memories flooded back to Robert as he walked up the drive towards the house. He recalled how his mother had taught him to ride a bike by pushing him down the sloping garden towards the beech hedge. It seemed a lifetime ago.

Continuing up the drive he could almost smell the barbecue and freshly cut grass as he walked past the sunken garden, a place his family would often have dined during hazy summer evenings. The sudden overload of emotion hit him hard and he took a couple of seconds to gather himself; wiping a solitary tear from his eye before stepping into the house.

Making his way down the hall Robert could hear a loud snoring sound coming from the living room. He glanced inside to see the prone figure of Charles in what appeared to be a very deep sleep. A sense of relief filled him as he wouldn't have to tell his father about the house until later. With this small mercy Robert turned on his heels and headed towards the kitchen.

The first thing he noticed was the glass on the counter containing a small dredge of whiskey. Robert understood why his father had been so sound asleep. He lifted the glass and walked over to the sink but as he neared the far side of the kitchen he failed to notice a protruding leg from the broken table. This caught his ankle, causing Robert to drop the glass. It smashed violently upon the tiled kitchen floor, spreading shards in every direction.

The tiled floor felt cold as Robert lowered onto his knees and started collecting the larger fragments. His eyes were then drawn to a white piece of paper lying crumpled upon the floor. He carefully disposed of the shards and then picked up the piece of paper to inspect it more closely. As he read his heart lifted and the sick feeling in the pit of his stomach began to subside. A sense of excitement, almost joy, filled Robert that he had not felt for some time. This would be a great challenge but in Robert's opinion this was an opportunity, or more accurately a lifeline, that they simply had to take.

Chapter Six

"No Robert, absolutely not, and that's final!"

Robert simply could not comprehend his father's objection. He had woken an hour ago and, in Robert's opinion, was harbouring a distinct lack of enthusiasm towards the letter.

"I've invited Hector over to discuss it, he'll be here shortly."

Robert hoped that Hector might help convince Charles of the merits of the plan, therefore negating the need for Robert to break the news they would soon be losing their house.

"Well you had no right to do that, so you best call him back and tell him not to bother."

"I can't do that. Besides, he'll be here any second."

Almost on cue there came a knock on the door.

"Bloody hell, that'll be him now. Well you'll have to entertain him for a while; I'm going to freshen up."

Charles scurried out of the room and up the stairs.

"Hello Robert. Might I say you look decidedly better than the last time I was here," quipped Hector as he stepped inside, removing his coat and scarf.

"Thanks, I actually haven't got round to fixing the table yet so if you could recommend a good carpenter that would be much appreciated. My father's just freshening up; could I offer you a cup of tea?"

Hector nodded as he set his coat and scarf down, carefully placing them over the back of a chair in the hallway. Robert led Hector to the kitchen and ushered him to take a seat as he filled the kettle.

"Blimey, I see what you mean about the table. What the hell happened Robert?"

"Let's just say my father isn't blessed with the calmest of tempers."

"I'd never have guessed," replied Hector, lifting his fringe to reveal the cut he sustained from Charles' recent bathroom attack.

"I'm sorry about that, and I'm sure my father is too. I actually never thanked you for trying to help me the other day but I want you to know that I appreciated what you did, and again I'm sorry my father lashed out at you."

"Don't mention it. You and I both know that Charles hasn't been himself for a very long time. He seems to have these self-destruct moments at the most inappropriate times, none more so than in the courtroom."

Hector placed his hand upon Robert's shoulder.

"You know if there was anything I could do to change Lord Stevens mind I would, but I'm afraid he's not likely to do so."

"That's fine."

Robert had now accepted his career as a solicitor was over.

"Before my father comes down I think you should know something. It's just that this opportunity you've presented, well, it's incredibly important for us."

Hector sensed from Robert's tone that this was a serious matter.

"You see, I went to the bank this morning and...."

"My, my, what have we here?"

Charles burst into the kitchen and extended his arm to shake hands with Hector. Robert immediately fell silent as Hector rose to accept the offer.

"Hector I'm very sorry that my son has troubled you by asking you to pay us a visit, I assure you I had no knowledge of this until a few moments ago."

"That's quite alright Charles, I'm always happy to pay you a visit, besides I believe you may be interested in the proposal as detailed in the letter."

Hector turned his focus towards Robert and nodded ever so slightly.

"To be quite honest Hector I have absolutely no interest in this. Like I said I'm sorry that Robert felt the need to bring you here but I assure you it will prove to be a wasted trip."

Robert felt the need to interject,

"Just here him out, please."

Robert motioned to Hector, encouraging him to speak. For his part Hector began to feel a little intimidated, not wanting to be the central figure in a family dispute.

"Um, well, as you will be aware the civil rights movement in America is seeking to enlist the help of legal experts in their fight against racial prejudices and has some limited success. This, they believe, will greatly assist in delivering on their agenda of social reforms by establishing equal legal rights for black citizens."

Hector could feel the glare of Charles' eyes upon him as he continued,

"The Dallas County Voters League is seeking to enlist a number of high profile Queen's Council representatives on a consultancy basis."

"Yes, yes Hector. I've read the details now please tell me what this has to do with me."

"Well, when the secretary contacted my office your name was mentioned as one of the QC's they'd be very keen to appoint."

"And?" snapped Charles.

"Well I just thought that if you were considering extending your legal career you may have to...."

"Have to what?" snarled Charles through squinted eyes.

"Seek new challenges," interjected Robert.

"Exactly," said Hector, happy to pounce on this interruption.

Charles seemed satisfied with this explanation but remained disinterested,

"To be quite honest Hector I couldn't give a damn about the civil rights movement in America."

"I understand," replied Hector, seemingly satisfied that he had tried his best to convince Charles, Robert would not give up so easily however.

"With your studying at Harvard you're sure to be a big catch for the Voters League. And I could be a member of your staff."

"Look Robert, I'm not listening to anymore of this nonsense."

"Nonsense? Is that what you think this is? Well in that case why don't you tell me where I can get another job as a solicitor?"

Hector sensed that a potentially explosive situation was beginning to develop.

"Look Robert, I'm sorry again for all that but we'll sort out something. I can have a word with Lord Stevens whenever he's calmed down."

"You know he's never going to change his mind. Hector was just telling me as much before you came down here."

Robert pointed at Hector who felt very uncomfortable being dragged into the argument again.

"Ok, fine, in that case I'll have a word with a few contacts and we'll get you set up in an accountancy firm in the city."

"I don't want to be an accountant. I know you probably can't understand this but all I ever wanted to do was to make my own way, but everywhere I turned people were always mentioning your name. Oh you're the son of.....I remember a case when your father.....everywhere I went your shadow went before me!" Robert could feel tears building.

"But then everything I worked for, all the effort I put in, it was finally starting to get me ahead on my own but you had to bring it to a crashing halt. So now where do I go? You owe me this chance!"

If Charles had felt any guilt over Robert's remarks he did not show it,

"You think I held you back? It was my name that got you where you are today so don't try and tell me that you've had it hard. I did everything I could to make it easy for you."

"Charles, Robert, please. There's no need to......

"Tell me exactly how you getting me excluded from practising is you 'making it easy for me'. Because to me that seems pretty difficult!"

"Look Robert, we're not going and that's final!" bellowed Charles as he rose to his feet.

"Yes we are," replied Robert, banging the worktop as he also stood up, "we have to!"

"Robert so help me I will never leave this house. This is the house that your mother and I spent the best years of our life in and I'll be damned if I'm to leave it."

"You have to leave it, there's nothing left here for you."

"It houses every memory your mother and I shared together, so don't you dare tell me there's nothing left here."

"We have to leave!"

"Why, why on earth do you have to leave?" Charles sensed something was not quite right.

"We have to leave because the bank is repossessing the house!"

The sentence hung in the air for a few seconds.

"Repossessed? They can't do that, besides I've plenty left in the savings to cover any payments."

Robert sat down again and placed his head in his hands,

"No.......no you don't."

"What do you mean I don't? Robert is there something you're not telling me?"

Hector was statuesque; he wanted to leave but couldn't find the right time to do so.

Robert's hands were trembling,

"I mean you don't have any savings because they're all gone."

"Gone?"

"Yes, gone" replied Robert, his gaze fixed upon the floor.

"How can that be?"

"Because......because........I lost it."

Tears were welling in Robert's eyes.

"Lost it?"

"Yes, lost it, it's all gone!"

"This must be some sort of joke."

"It's all gone!" exclaimed Robert, emphasising this was definitely not a joke.

"What the hell have you done Robert?"

Robert lifted his stare from the floor and looked into his father's eyes, but what he saw did not seem to offer him any comfort.

"I didn't mean to. At the start I thought I could use your savings to generate a little extra cash. Heaven knows you hadn't been working for some time and I was struggling to keep up with all our payments so I invested the savings in shares that I was told were sure to increase substantially. But the market never reacted as it was supposed to; before I knew it the value of the shares had plummeted. I tried to take them out but they had decreased so much that by the time I did they were almost worthless."

Charles' eyes were wide open and he could feel the anger growing inside him.

"So how much is left?"

"Well, when I realised just how much I'd lost I panicked. I took all that was left with me to the Blackthorn pub.

"So you drank the rest of it away?"

"No, there was a poker game on. I thought that I could win back everything I lost, but......"

"You lost the lot!"

Charles slumped back down into his chair as the realisation and consequences of Robert's actions slowly dawned on him.

"When did you go to the Blackthorn?"

Robert exhaled loudly.

"The day we got thrown out of court."

"So you're telling me that my house is to be taken away from me?"

Charles' voice was becoming louder as he continued,

"And everything I worked so hard for, is all gone?"

"I'm sorry father, I never meant to......"

"Don't say another word Robert!" Charles snapped.

"Charles if there is anything at all I can do to help please...."

Charles silenced Hector with a deathly stare.

"I think it would be best if you gave me and my son some privacy Hector. Thank you for stopping by, I trust you can see yourself out."

"Ok, but remember if there's anything I can do."

Hector didn't wait for a response as he gathered his coat and scarf and left.

As the door slammed shut Charles turned to Robert,

"You bloody fool! How could you be so stupid? So selfish?"

Robert's heart was pounding as his father continued with his vicious tirade.

"I can't believe what you've done!"

"I'm sorry I..."

"Get out of my sight!" blasted Charles.

Robert slowly motioned towards the door and turned to face his father before he left.

"I didn't mean to..."

"Get out you bloody fool!"

With that Robert left the room and the house entirely.

Charles felt crushed. Inside he was a mixture of emotions; primarily he was angry but he was also harbouring a dull sickness in his stomach. Charles knew this stemmed from the thought of having to tear himself away from the reminders of his marriage contained within the house. He began to weep as painful memories came flooding back. As this tsunami of emotional heartache washed over him a voice inside Charles' head convinced him he wasn't strong enough to handle the situation. And as was typical, Charles set about making the pain stop.

Charles hurried to the drinks cabinet in the kitchen and poured a tall glass of whiskey, spilling some plenty as he frantically poured. He lifted the glass to his lips and took three large mouthfuls before refilling the glass.

'Soon the pain will be over', he told himself, and as the whiskey penetrated his blood stream Charles began to feel comfortably numb, a feeling he had become well accustomed to.

Chapter Seven

The biting wind penetrated Robert to the core as he walked through the cemetery gates. He hadn't been there for so long that he forgot which one of the pathways to take. However he eventually regained his bearings and began circumnavigating his way through the maze of grief and sorrow. As he walked he found himself captivated by the inscriptions upon the gravestones; each contained only a brief message but to those that hold the belief and share the pain it would mean infinitely more.

His eyes were drawn to what appeared quite a new gravestone. It displayed the message 'April is the cruellest month'. He recognised the quotation as being from T.S Eliot's 'The Waste Land', having studied it at school some years ago. He paused to recall other poignant verses, 'and the dead tree gives no shelter, the cricket no relief, and the dry stone no sound of water'. Robert was not fond of the piece when he was younger but now, having felt able to connect with it, he held it in much higher regard. He stooped to read the details of the inscription – 'In loving memory of our son, David Robson, died aged 16.' As Robert rose he thought back to being sixteen and how young and invincible he felt, before the harshness of the world had caught up with him.

A light drizzle began to fall as Robert followed the pathway up the hill. A middle-aged man was accompanying an elderly woman down the slope and he greeted Robert with a silent nod as they crossed. Robert replicated the gesture and continued on his way, conscious that the bunch of flowers he was carrying was a cheaper option than the vast array of floral arrangements that colourfully decorated this part of the graveyard. However the contrast between the bright petals and grey headstones served to remind Robert of the distinction between that which was living and that which was dead.

The rain was now falling heavily as Robert approached his destination. It had caused his wet locks to break free from the shackles of their styling. On the previous occasions Robert had been here since the funeral he never knew what to feel and once again he was full of conflicting emotions as he arrived at his mother's grave. Seeing her full name displayed before him seemed to make his being there less personal, giving it a more formal feel. Robert laid the flowers down by the headstone and as he did so he tried to conjure a mental picture of his mother. He struggled at first to visualise her without seeing how she appeared during her final few hours, unconscious in a hospital bed sustained only by a series of tubes. Robert could still hear the beeping of the heart monitor, the only signal of life. He remembered how he had wished desperately for the beep to increase its rate and for her to return his squeeze of her hand, but it never happened. For three years since Robert had been haunted by that cruel, incessant beep.

As the pain began to swell inside Robert cleared his head and tried to remember happier times. He transported himself back to his kitchen, watching his mother and father dancing to jazz music playing on the radio. Their faces were of pure delight and full of admiration for each other, oblivious to the decreasing joyous occasions life would afford them to spend together. Robert began to weep as he recalled his father twirling his mother before they landed in a heap on the settee, giddy as two teenage lovers. They stepped perfectly in time in a dance they believed would have lasted much longer.

Robert bent down and, staring at his mother's name before him, he sobbed uncontrollably. All the emotion of the past few days had finally caught up with him. Previously it would've been his mother that Robert would've confided in and now, even in death, he could not help but open his heart to her. Robert began to speak softly through the tears,

"I'm sorry" he whispered under his breath.

"It's so tough without you. I....I'm trying, I really am, but it's so hard."

Robert wiped the tears from his eyes and removed a handkerchief from his pocket. This composed him slightly and he glanced to make sure no-one had witnessed his outburst. He took a deep breath as he remembered the reason for his visit and once again knelt down.

"Mother, I love you dearly and always will," Robert spoke softly, with calm determination.

"I came here to tell you something. We can no longer stay in the family house. The reason for this is my fault and I will carry the shame and guilt with me all my life. But I also know I have to get father out of there. He misses you so much and hasn't been able to cope."

Robert could feel the lump in his throat returning.

"I've tried my best to help him, honestly I have, but I don't think I'll ever get through. But I've come to promise you that I will look after him, at least until he is capable of handling himself. We have to leave the country and.........I don't know if we will ever make it back. But just because we may not visit this grave doesn't mean that you won't be with us. I know you're by my side everywhere I go and I'm sorry for the way I've let the family down. I pray that I can make you proud of me and I ask God to grant me strength to do this."

Once again the tears began to flow freely.

"Now I have to leave this place.......but I will look after him I swear. And I swear I will make you proud of me."

Robert pressed his fingers to his mouth and kissed them before touching the cold gravestone. He got up and turned sharply to head back down the hill, unaware that the rain had thoroughly soaked him as he left his mother's graveside.

****

Charles' stomach muscles strained with every painful heave as his body attempted to purge itself of the whiskey it had been subjected to last night. Tears were streaming from his eyes as his stomach tensed once again but there was nothing left inside to remove besides stomach bile; the foul-tasting, pale yellow liquid causing Charles to gag as he loudly heaved once more. With his stomach now vacant and aching he straightened up and looked at himself in the bathroom mirror. After removing some saliva from his mouth and chin he splashed cold water on his face to try and revive himself. He felt weak and weary as he lay back down upon his bed, contemplating the news that Robert had delivered the day before. His first instinct was to refuse to leave the house but his more realistic side, the one which he could not silence with alcohol, told him that he knew his time in the house was coming to an end.

Charles was angry and keen to continue his chastisement of his son but in rising from the bed he clumsily bumped into the bedside table and knocked a number of items onto the floor. Bending over led to a sudden head rush so Charles dropped onto his knees to pick up the pieces. A pair of glasses, two books and a clock were returned to their original place. Charles was about to get back up when he noticed a photograph, face down, which still lay on the floor. He reached for it and turned the photo to reveal an image of him and Sarah on holiday. It was taken many years ago, when Robert was only 12. Charles had been using this as a bookmark for a piece of legal fiction he had been reading a few years ago, before his wife became ill. The discovery of a reminder of the past usually led Charles to seek comfort from a bottle but, with his stomach still aching, he couldn't face the prospect of abusing it once again so he had no choice but to face reality.

Surveying the photo brought back a world of memories but as Charles sat on the edge of the bed he focused only upon Robert, who was waving and smiling proudly at the camera. His excitement and care-free abandon led to a feeling of guilt. The longer Charles stared, the more certain truths became apparent to him. Robert was his only son and began a legal career solely to follow in his footsteps and now

Charles had taken that away from him. Slowly any lingering feelings of anger towards Robert melted away as he contemplated his recent reckless behaviour. How tough this must've been upon Robert, Charles mused, becoming more guilt-ridden with every flashback. He was then met with a deep sense of shame as his eyes moved to focus upon Sarah. Charles knew he had let her down.

******

Robert was apprehensive as he returned home. He had witnessed many bouts of rage from his father recently and was not looking forward to being subjected to another. He was therefore very surprised to hear Charles greet him in a calm and pleasant manner as he entered the kitchen.
"Hello Robert. How are you?"
 "I'm ok, all things considered. Father, I'm so sorry I...."
"Robert it is I who have let you down," said Charles with a sigh.
"You had both our best interests at heart which is the important thing."
Robert was dumbfounded by Charles' behaviour and had a quick glance towards the kitchen counter to see if Charles had been drinking.
"Look son, I know it's going to be tough leaving this house behind but there's nothing can be done to change that now. And perhaps a change of scenery may do us both some good. I've spoken with Hector and am expecting a call later this afternoon from the Dallas County Voters League to discuss the position. Could I please ask you to remain in the house in case they call before I return, I have a couple of matters to attend to."
"Absolutely. Can I ask what you are doing, perhaps I can help?"
"Thank you for the offer but I believe these matters will require my personal attention. Firstly I need to get a reference from a senior QC so will be paying a visit to Lord Kitchener, then I must call into the bank to sign a couple of documents and formalise the deed transfer."
Robert felt strangely comforted to see Charles acting in a responsible manner for the first time in a very long time. And as his father left the room Robert began to get excited about the prospect of America and the opportunities that awaited him there.
     As he left the room Charles felt satisfied with the performance he had displayed. He had depicted a calm demeanour which belied his nervous and indeed tormented emotional state. He had also neglected to mention the main priority he

had to take care during the next couple of hours. It seemed Sarah's grave had not witnessed its last visitor of the day.

Chapter Eight

A wall of heat greeted Robert as he stepped off the plane. Having developed a fear of flying following a turbulent flight to France a few years ago he found the nine hour crossing a nerve-gangling experience, made no easier by the fact his fear prevented him from sleeping. Charles suffered no such difficulties and after two large whiskeys was out cold until they touched down at Birmingham International Airport.

As they walked from the plane to the terminal building Robert was full of excitement and relief. The anxiety which had been growing inside with each bump and vibration the plane underwent was now flowing from him. He was almost giddy. Charles was less enthusiastic; he had not yet woken up and found the combination of a fuzzy head and simmering heat unbearable. His mouth was dry and he desperately needed a drink. He had been given a description by Hector of the person who would be greeting them but rather than meet him now Charles decided to freshen up and so made his way to the bathroom. Oblivious to his father's discomfort Robert continued down the corridor to the baggage reclaim, still full of contentment at being safely back on the ground.

After some time Charles entered the baggage reclaim area to find Robert had already gathered both their suitcases from the carousel. The airport was hot and the heady bustle of people coming and going seemed to add to the temperature. Charles could feel himself sweating as he followed Robert towards the exit. Desperate for some fresh air and breathing space, Charles burst through the doors but found the temperature outside warmer than in the building. There was no fresh air on offer either; the occasional breeze adding to the heat by bringing a surge of warm air upon him.

Robert studied a map of the airport to find the designated meeting point while Charles sat on a nearby bench, fanning a newspaper in his face in an attempt to cool down. Charles removed a sweater from across his shoulders and placed it inside his suitcase, embarrassed that he had even contemplated the need to wear it. As he sat Charles surveyed the scene around him. A procession of taxis was constantly pulling up to drop off expectant travellers or to collect weary ones, while people were marching in all directions. Everyone appeared to be talking louder, shouting at each other. Cars also seemed noisier with a constant barrage of horns beeping in anger and frustration. In fact everything seemed louder than back home, operating at a faster, more frantic pace.

"Ok, we have to make our way to Area C3 which is about 200 yards this direction," said Robert, breaking Charles' fascination with all that was transpiring around him.

"Very well, lead on in that case."

Charles was struggling to keep pace with Robert as he proceeded down the footpath. He was worried Robert had already tuned into this faster way of life, but in reality he was just full of nervous energy from the flight. A large sign clearly highlighted Area C3 but there was no-one waiting there. Once again the offer of a bench was too appealing for Charles and he sat down to gather his breath. He reached into his bag and removed a bottle of water. It had been cold when he bought it but by now was look-warm, severely reducing its ability to quench Charles' thirst. Regardless, he gulped down three large mouthfuls before offering a drink to Robert. Robert seemed distracted and fidgety; ignoring Charles' offer as he tried to identify the person they were scheduled to meet. After a couple of minutes he too sat down on the bench and lifted Charles' bottle of water from the pavement. He took one sip and spat it out.

"You might have told me it was warm."

"I thought you'd figure that out yourself. Well, where is this chap?"

"I don't know. Perhaps our flight was in a bit early. Let's just wait here until he appears."

The air was a still, dead heat; the light breeze having now vanished. In this moment of relatively peace and quiet, Robert sought to find out exactly what Charles was being expected to provide;

"Do you know roughly what work you will be doing? And do you think I'll be able to help?"

"To be honest I'm not completely sure of my role. The chap on the phone mentioned some details but I'm a little rusty on American law. However I'm sure I'll be able to reacquaint myself quickly."

Charles's response had not filled Robert with much confidence but before he could contemplate the situation he heard the rumbling sound of a noisy diesel engine approaching. The two men watched silently as a dated-looking, beige Ford pulled up alongside them, bellowing thick black smoke from the exhaust. A strong smell of diesel penetrated the still air as a short, plump figure emerged from the driver's side. Without breaking eye contact with Charles he opened the passenger door, allowing a taller, slimmer man to step out of the car.

"Mr Ainsworth I presume?" said the man as he stretched out his hand to greet Charles.

Although he knew he would be working for a black civil rights group, it hadn't actually dawned on Charles until now that he would be meeting a black man, and as Charles shook his hand he was dumbstruck. He shook without replying, trying desperately to remember the name Hector had given him but his mind was drawing a blank.

"Nice to meet you," he offered, eventually.

"And, um, allow me to introduce my son, this is Robert."

Robert stepped forward to shake the man's hand, conscious that his father hadn't offered the man's name during the introduction.

"Nice to meet you Robert, Hector has told me all about you. My name is Jim Alder; it is very good of you to come with your father."

"Alder" thought Charles, silently chastising himself for forgetting this vital detail. Robert studied Mr Alder's face as he shook his hand. He was a relatively old man, in the region of 60 or thereabouts Robert guessed. His dark hair was now greying around the edges and the skin on his face looked tough as a piece of leather. But he had a friendly demeanour, sympathetic eyes and a warm smile as he greeted Robert.

"I trust you had a pleasant flight?"

"Yes, very good, although long," replied Robert, deciding not to mention that it had been amongst the longest nine hours of his life.

"As long as y'all made it safely, that's the most important thing I suppose. We do have some more travelling ahead of us today but it shouldn't take too long."

"That's quite alright Mr Alder," said Charles, hoping that the use of the name implied that he had known this all along.

"Please, call me Jim."

"Very well Jim, so long as you call me Charles."

The two men nodded approvingly to each other as the driver finished placing the luggage in the car.

"We are ready now so if you would please get into the car, we do have a long drive ahead," said the driver, maintaining his strange glare at Charles.

As the car noisily trundled through the airport traffic system and onto the freeway, Robert felt his eyes getting very heavy. He was determined to fight the temptation to sleep as he wanted to take in his new surroundings but as the sound of conversation within the car grew fainter he succumbed to a deep slumber.

Having noticed Robert fall asleep Charles felt uncomfortable. He knew he would now be expected to maintain conversation alone. He was still unnerved by his new surroundings and this, combined with his poor first impression and the unnerving glare from the driver made him uncomfortable. 'If only I could have a drink', he thought, 'just to calm my nerves and make me more sociable'.

This was how his addiction started, alcohol offering a supposed helping hand but somewhere along the line it changed to dependence.

"Jim could we please put a window down?"

"No problem. The heat is something you will have to get used to."

"Indeed," replied Charles, dismissing this comment as nonsense. His dry tone seemed to agitate the driver and Charles noticed his large dark eyes staring at him in the rear view mirror.

"Um, I mean I certainly hope so."

This seemed to satisfy the driver who returned his attention to the road again.

*****

The farther away from city they travelled the more Charles noticed their surroundings deteriorate. He had been astounded by the tall skyscrapers that dominated the city skyline; each making him feel small and insignificant but these tall giants, the frantic pace of the airport and the freeway now didn't seem quite as daunting as the car noisily passed through a series of smaller towns, each containing a high proportion of vacant stores and dilapidated buildings. The smooth surface of the freeway and main roads had also given way to a crater-laden track that offered up clouds of dust with every bump the car went over; a particularly violent one of which saw Robert jolt out of his sleep and back into consciousness. He was groggy and disorientated as he rubbed his eyes, squinting to help them adjust to the bright sunshine. A small pool of saliva had trickled down his chin, leaving a mark on his cream shirt. Robert was embarrassed at discovering this but the furnace-like heat inside the car would soon dissolve any trace of the stain.

"How long was I out?"

"Good hour or thereabouts I'd say. Don't worry, we ain't got too much further to go," replied Jim.

Charles was worried. He had watched with growing concern as outside the environment becoming steadily less affluent and now they were nearly at their final destination he was greatly perturbed. Studying Robert's face as he took in the changed scenery, Charles also detected the same sense of apprehension in his son. Robert sensed he was being watched and turned to find Charles staring directly at him. The two men communicated a mutual feeling of at best being underwhelmed and as worst being genuinely worried, until a jovial comment from Jim broke their concentration.

"Ain't no place like home."

The car pulled up in the driveway and came to rest at the side of a white wooden building. Jim's comment could not have been more apt as Charles thought about his home back in London. The meandering driveway and rolling garden leading to a magnificent Georgian town house boasting a vast array of luxuries and comforts. By comparison the modest, run-down residence in front of them would not have been suitable as an outhouse on his previous property.

"This should be to your liking," quipped Jim.

His constant good nature was starting to irritate Charles.

"It seems somewhat.......rustic," replied Charles.

"In a quaint sort of way," added Robert, aware that this was their new employer he was addressing.

"Yep, suppose it is kinda quaint."

Jim stepped back to take in the full view of the house, as if viewing the property in a new light following Robert's description. He hadn't detected any negativity in Charles' mood but once again the driver was keeping a close watch on him as he pulled the car on a halt and began lifting the suitcases from the trunk.

"Please, let me give you a hand with those," said Robert.

"And sorry, I didn't catch your name earlier."

"Pardon me Robert, that's my fault. This here is Mr Benson; he provides a number of services for us at the Voters League."

There was no offer of a handshake as he continued lifting the bags from the boot of the car. Robert picked up one and set it down on the lawn.

"Tell me Mr Benson, what services do you provide?"

Robert studied the short stocky figure in front of him, trying to catch his eye.

"Security," he replied dryly.

The steps up to the front decking area creaked under Charles's feet as he climbed. He wanted to inspect the premises on his own, leaving Robert and Mr Benson to sort out the luggage, but another creaking sound behind him indicated that Jim was following.

"Hold on Charles and I'll get that front door for you now."

The initial glass front door was open but it took Jim a couple of tries to find the correct key for the main front door. Eventually he found a key that the lock accepted and after encountering some slight resistance from the now unlocked door he barged it open with his shoulder.

"The door is a little stiff but you can soon see to that."

Charles did not reply as he stepped inside his new home. Jim led him down a narrow corridor and into an open space which served as a combined kitchen and living area. Charles' sense of disappointment was palpable as he surveyed the room. The furniture in the living area side appeared worn out and dirty, while the kitchen was far too small in Charles' opinion to allow space for anyone to attempt to cook a meal. The antiquated oven also didn't inspire much confidence.

The wallpaper was the next offending item; it was faded and was starting to come off the wall in the corners of the room. This, Charles presumed, was an indication of dampness or more likely in this heat, inadequate plumbing upstairs.

Having failed to impress Charles with the first room Jim led him to the main bedroom. Charles remained silent but was apprehensive as he entered. To his surprise he was relieved to find the room was in quite good condition; a large master bed dominated the space, supported by a matching closet, bedside table and set of drawers.

"This will be my room I feel," said Charles, chirpily.

"Ah yes, I hoped you'd like it," replied Jim, happy that Charles now felt comfortable enough to speak.

"If you would follow me I'll now show you the second bedroom, or should that be Robert's room?"

"Ah yes, please lead on."

Robert's room was significantly smaller but also looked to be in a reasonable condition, as did the bathroom which Jim showed to Charles afterwards. Charles couldn't help but think that Jim would've been much wiser to show him any of these rooms first.

"That's the luggage in," grunted Mr Benson, "we best be off Mr Alder as there are things need a-doing."

"Yes, indeed. Well, I hope y'all will see to making yourselves at home here. I'll send a car tomorrow afternoon to give you a tour of the local area and show you the offices you'll be working at. Now I'm sorry but we really must get going."

Jim shook hands with Charles before turning to follow Mr Benson down the hall. He also said a rushed goodbye to Robert as they met on the corridor.

"Where are they off to in such a hurry?" asked Robert as he joined Charles at the end of the hall.

"I don't know, but we'll see them again tomorrow. You haven't been round the house yet have you?"

"No, I've been sorting *our* luggage."

"Well in that case I'll give you the full tour. Firstly, let me show you to your room."

Chapter Nine

"As the marchers crossed the Edmund Pettus Bridge they were ordered to disband by the awaiting state troopers. Within seconds scuffles broke out. Demonstrators were beaten to the ground with nightsticks and tear gas was fired into the crowd. Mounted troopers confronted the demonstrators on horseback as....."

It was 1965 and Robert listened intently to the local radio news broadcasts. The first incident had been termed 'Bloody Sunday', where protestors marked the death of Jimmie Lee Jackson and the second march had taken place the following Tuesday. It had been televised and had presented the world with images of marchers left bloodied and severely injured, seventeen of which had been hospitalised.

He was fascinated by the escalating situation and wanted to understand how tensions had become so frayed. Living a sheltered life in England he heard little and didn't care much about the civil rights movement in America, but now he had been cast into the middle of it he was engrossed.

By contrast Charles did not consider the simmering tensions intriguing. The visit to the offices, organised by Jim the day after they arrived, highlighted how little money and facilities the Dallas County Voters League had. A brief meeting with the staff also indicated how much faith they had in his legal ability. Many of the volunteers mentioned 'Jim Crow' but the term did not resonate with him. This led to awkward moments of bluffing as Charles tried to convince the staff he was fully versed on the issue and could challenge the laws. Upon leaving he immediately instructed Robert to prepare a full briefing on current legislation and Jim Crow so that he wouldn't be caught out again.

Robert had a spring in his step as he left the house towards the University law library. Despite previously not being interested he was now glad to be actively involved in the fight for civil justice; this wasn't because of a sense of moral conscience or indignation but rather he was relieved to have a distraction to occupy his mind. His thoughts had recently turned towards his old life in England and the mother he so desperately missed.

The day had only just dawned but already Robert was finding it uncomfortably warm. He slipped off his jacket and casually tossed it over his shoulder as he continued down the road to the bus stop. Arriving as the number 49 bus did likewise, Robert stepped onboard and made his way to one of the few remaining free seats towards the back. Perhaps it was his imagination but Robert got the feeling he was being watched. Where possible he studied the faces of his fellow travellers, shifting his gaze from the floor as often as he felt comfortable in doing so. On each occasion he was confronted by a set of steely, dark eyes, staring directly at him. The eyes in question belonged to a tall young man with a messy flock of dirty blonde hair. He was seated on the back row of the bus, chewing gum loudly and his eyes narrowed slightly each time Robert turned around to glance his direction. After three such incidents he was convinced this was no coincidence and began to perspire as he sat motionless in his seat. His eyes were fixed firmly ahead but he could feel the young man's stare penetrating the back of his head. Robert couldn't understand why he was the subject of such attention and contemplated getting off. However, his thoughts were disturbed by the 'stop' bell sound. The bus driver obliged the passenger's request and signalled to pull over. As he did so the young man noisily rose to his feet and started making his way down the aisle. Robert's heart was pounding as he stared directly at the floor; each approaching footstep filling him with a sense of dread. Robert continued to gaze down but with his peripheral vision he sensed the young man had stopped just behind him. Robert was shaking, unsure what to expect to happen next. Then, after a matter of seconds, but what seemed much longer, the young man set off again down the aisle. As he saw the man leave the bus Robert exhaled loudly. The driver signalled to rejoin the traffic and Robert watched the young man head off down the road. A sense of relief washed over him, followed by a one of embarrassment as he contemplated how ridiculous his suspicions had been. He then lifted his newspaper and set about trying to relax for the duration of the journey. As if to finally draw a line under the incident he looked out the window at the young man. He noticed he had a large scar on his face and his heart began racing again as the young man held Robert's gaze. Without blinking he lifted his hand to run his thumb across his throat in a cutting motion. The sick feeling returned to the pit of Robert's stomach.

*****

Having sent Robert out on his fact-finding mission Charles was unsure how to spend his day. He decided to go into town and find his bearings of the local area. He was going to afford himself the luxury of a long shower but there was a lack of warm water so Charles had to make do with a lukewarm one instead. Regardless of this he followed it with a relaxing early lunch, meaning it was near midday by the time he ventured outside into the Alabama heat.

Having not made a good first impression with his new employers Charles thought it prudent to call in today and try to redeem himself. He was not scheduled to start working until the start of the following week so visiting now would show both his dedication and professionalism.

It was quite a long walk into town and as Charles baked in the midday sun he regretted not getting a bus. When he arrived at the office Charles had suffered so much at the hands of the elements that his once pristine shirt was now drenched in sweat. He was exhausted and knew to arrive in this condition would not rectify his previous bad appearance. Instead he decided to call into a nearby cafe to have a drink and a rest.

Charles stepped inside to be greeted by the refreshing sensation of cold air, courtesy of the air conditioning unit. He savoured the feeling for a few seconds before taking a seat at an unoccupied table. The cafe looked dated and in need of repair but as Charles wasn't hungry he felt it would suffice as somewhere to quench his thirst. He perused the menu, awaiting the arrival of a waitress to take his order, but with none forthcoming he began surveying the cafe's clientele. There was a mixture of people within the shop, young and old, men and women but the most striking divide was between the black and white customers. Each sat in what Charles presumed to be their own designated area. It was then Charles noticed he was sitting in the midst of the black customers. Unaware of what to do, he sat there pondering his options. If he got up and joined the white side he risked offending the black guests, whereas the longer he sat where he was the more he might offend the white customers. His internal dilemma was interrupted by the arrival of the waitress. She was a young girl with dark skin, sleek black hair and seemed ill at ease with Charles' choice of seating.

"Chef says you might be better sitting over there," said the girl, gingerly.

Charles panicked. He had never held any particular racist views but would soon be working for a voting rights group for blacks. He decided to stay put.

"I'm fine here, thank you. May I just have some water?"

The girl looked worried and left without saying a word.

As he sat there Charles felt exposed, like he was being studied by everyone. Occasionally he caught a glance from some of his fellow diners but no-one afforded him a smile. Charles began to feel increasingly awkward and could feel his cheeks redden, somehow impervious to the cool air being dispensed by the air conditioning.

"You the England man come to help?"

Charles turned to find an old woman at the next table staring directly at him through a thick pair of glasses.

"Uh, yes...... I am indeed," replied Charles as softly as possible.

"Well thank the Lord, I sure hope you can help us," responded the woman enthusiastically. Her loud voice caught the attention of most of the customers in the cafe, who were now staring intently at the exchange.

"Well, I'll do my best," said Charles sharply. He wanted to end the conversation as he could feel his hands beginning to tremor.

The waitress returned with a tall glass of water. She silently left it on the table and turned to serve another customer. Charles lifted the glass to his lips and drank it down quick. He then produced two dollars and threw it down on the table before making a quick exit.

"Make sure and come back now," offered the old woman.

Charles didn't look back as he stepped outside into the heat.

Charles was on edge. He felt all the customers were still watching him as he strode down the street. Just as luck would have it he looked up to see a 'welcome' sign. 'I'll just have one drink to help me relax', and with that he was gone.

The small establishment was called Bob's. The buzzing neon sign outside indicated the bar was open, although in the bright sunlight it was difficult to tell. Charles stepped inside and was relieved to find it practically empty. He sat at a stool at the end of the bar and ordered a large scotch.

"We don't have scotch, bourbon okay?"

"It will have to do," muttered Charles.

The barman took the bottle from the shelf and poured a tall glass before setting it down in front of Charles.

"You new in town?"

Charles ignored him as he took a sip from the glass. The bourbon was even rougher than the whiskey, like sandpaper on the back of his throat.

Undeterred, the barman continued;

"I said, you new to these parts?"

Charles sensed it would be impossible to ignore the questions.

"I'm here from London.......for a fixed period of work."

"What line of work you in?"

"None of your business."

"Ok, ok, I'll leave you be. I have to sort out a few things out the back anyways. Anything else I can get you before I go?"

"Just leave the bottle," said Charles as he stared into his now empty glass.

"Now mister are you sure....."

"I said just leave it!"

"Ok, be my guest."

"Much obliged," whispered Charles, his head and shoulders hunched in shame. With that the barman made his exit, leaving Charles alone to contemplate the recent events that had led him to this point. And when it all became too much he made himself comfortably numb once again.

*****

Robert walked briskly from the library to the bus stop. The incident earlier in the day was still playing on his mind; in fact he had found it difficult to focus on anything else. He kept replaying the scene again and again, each time asking 'how could anyone know who I am' and, more importantly, 'why would they want to hurt me?' On the rare occasions when he had managed to concentrate he had gathered some useful background information on Jim Crow, but felt he hadn't achieved what he set out to.

As the bus appeared Robert began to panic, worrying that the young man from earlier on would be waiting for him. As he gingerly stepped aboard he was relieved to find the bus empty and the man not there. Robert sat in the fourth row and placed his satchel on the seat beside him, preventing anyone sitting down next to him. The engine juddered loudly and as the driver shut the doors Robert stared vacantly out the window. He watched as the large vehicle cascaded through the dusty countryside; past fields desperate for rain and dilapidated shops begging for customers; neither of which had had their wishes granted for some time.

The bus had obediently completed most of the stops on its route. As it approached what was due to be Robert's penultimate stop he noticed a familiar looking character sitting outside a bar. Robert sprang to his feet and darted off the bus as soon as the doors opened, carrying his satchel in one hand. He sprinted over and grabbed the person by the shoulder, making them turn to face him in one abrupt movement.

"What are you doing here?"

"I....I.....I came to find my way about the town," slurred Charles clumsily, struggling to focus upon Robert as his left eye was now practically shut.

"Right well, we're leaving!"

"I'm not going anywhere."

"Listen you fool, if anyone sees you here in this condition we'll be finished."

"I just want to enjoy a quiet drink, is that too much to ask?" snapped Charles, with growing irritation evident in his tone.

"You've already had a quiet drink, now it's time to go home."
Robert stood over Charles and, putting his arms below Charles's, he tried to lift him up. Charles was outraged by this manhandling and shrugged his shoulders violently to release himself from Robert's grasp, accidentally knocking over the half-empty bottle in the process. Charles broke free and as the liquid flowed from the bottle he was furious. Robert could see the burning rage in Charles's eyes but before he could act he was caught by a vicious right hook to the face. This rocked him back on his heels and Charles followed up with a volley of punches to Robert's midriff, each one connecting perfectly with his son's ribs. Desperate for some respite Robert grabbed Charles and delivered a knee into his stomach. The blow hurt Charles but he had adrenalin coursing through his veins and before the pain set in he sprang towards Robert, tackling him to the ground. The two men wrestled on the floor, with a series of inaccurate punches failing to find their mark as both tried to suppress the other. Charles was tiring but in a desperate last stand he delivered a crushing head butt, shattering Robert's nose into a bloodied mess. With Robert momentarily incapacitated Charles, without thinking, lifted the bourbon bottle. He brought it down towards Robert's head but a hand grabbed his wrist, preventing him from striking. Charles turned to find that the hand belonged to a young woman. Shocked, he looked down at Robert; his face already swollen and covered in blood. He then looked at the bottle in his hand and a sense of shame engulfed him. He dropped the bottle and silently, tearfully fled the scene.

  Robert lay on the ground, dazed. He had been expecting another blow but opening his eyes he was shocked to find a woman tending to him instead. She had smooth dark skin and a gentle touch as she wiped the blood from his face. His nose, cheek and eye were aching but as he lay there he felt comforted. Robert strained his eyes in the evening sunlight to see the woman more clearly. She was black, had long, sleek hair, dark welcoming eyes and a warm smile. Robert was awestruck by her beauty and stared at her intently. After a few seconds the young woman began to blush and looked away, snapping Robert out of his infatuated glare. Suddenly the pain returned to his face and body, signalling that her comfort spell had ended. As if to confirm this fact she told him 'hold still, this will hurt'. Before he could contemplate the instruction the woman placed her thumbs either side of the bridge of his nose and jolted it sharply back into place. Robert let out a loud yell and was immediately embarrassed by his reaction. Sensing this embarrassment the woman gave a playful smirk.
"What did you do to make that guy so angry?"
"I told him to stop drinking."

"Looks like he didn't want your advice."

"What can I say; you don't choose your father."

With that Robert sat up and was greeted with a thumping pain in his head.

"Which way did he go?"

"He made off down that street. You're not thinking about going after him now are you?"

Robert rose to his feet and dusted himself off.

"I have to."

"He was about to smash you over the head with a bottle!".

"Listen, I have to look after him. I'm the only family he's got."

Robert turned to walk after him but became light-headed. He could feel a cool sweat on his brow and the energy draining from his legs as they began to buckle under him. He couldn't be sure but the last thing he saw before it went dark was the face of an angel rushing towards him.

Chapter Ten

"Well, how you feeling this morning?"

As he laid in a soft bed the sentence penetrated Robert's subconscious until eventually he stirred. He looked around but did not recognise the room. Robert tried to rub his eyes but the swelling made them sensitive to the touch and he grimaced with pain.

"You'd be best not doing that," said a voice from within the room.

Robert sat up to find the young woman sat at the foot of his bed.

"Where am I?"

"You're at my place. You passed out so I thought I better take you home to make sure you're okay. You slept right through the night; I guess you took quite a beat down."

Robert gently touched his face.

"I forgot my father used to be an amateur boxer. Thank you for your hospitality......sorry, I don't even know your name."

"It's Sophia. And the reason I know yours is because I gathered up your bag to bring back."

"You brought my stuff? I don't know what I can do to repay you."

Robert was about to get out of the bed when he discovered that he was only wearing a pair of boxer shorts.

"Did you..........did you undress me?"

"Well, eh.......yes I had to. I mean, your clothes were awfully dirty, what with the dust and blood."

Robert could tell Sophia was embarrassed.

"So this is what you do, bring home complete strangers and undress them?"

"Well it was either that or leave you to get *another* beating."

"*And* I did go to the trouble of washing your clothes. But if you'd rather I hadn't then you're free to take them off the line. I don't think they'll be dry but at least you'll have your dignity. Now while you wait for your clothes how about some breakfast. I'll make it and in the meantime you can have a shower and freshen up."

"Sounds good."

"Ok, I'll bring you a fresh towel, a t-shirt and pair of my dad's old trousers. They're not too fashionable mind."

With that Sophia left the room, leaving Robert's heart aflutter. He knew practically nothing about this woman but spending these few minutes with her had been the most enjoyable thing he could remember for a very long time.

*****

Charles's hand and head were both throbbing; dancing to the same painful beat. His mouth was as dry as the dusty road outside while his memory was hazy like the early morning sunshine. He had a feeling that something bad had happened but couldn't be sure what.

The pain in his head was unrelenting as he climbed out of bed and made his way to the bathroom. He was shocked to find a series of cuts and grazes to his head and moved towards the mirror for a closer inspection. It was then he noticed his swollen right knuckles. He studied his hand, trying desperately to recall or imagine the actions that had led to this. Slowly a series of flashbacks from the day before began trickling back. He remembered the cool air of the cafe. His next recollection was of buying bourbon, the stale aftertaste he was still experiencing. Someone then grabbed him and tried to lift him, spilling his drink. There was an argument, raised voices, punches, he remembered being on the floor, he remembered grabbing a bottle but didn't know whether he used it or not. Then finally, the sickening sting of the final flashback – he remembered, it was Robert.

*****

The smell of fried bacon filled the house as Robert got dressed. He had taken a long time in the bathroom trying to make himself look as good as possible, which was proving difficult in the old clothes he was wearing. Robert made one final adjustment to his hair before taking a deep breath and stepping into the kitchen.
"My my, don't you look handsome?"
Robert was caught off guard and could feel his cheeks beginning to redden.
"Eh, thanks....I'm not sure about the colour."
"Oh I think it suits you fine. Now sit down and I'll bring this over."
Robert pulled up a chair at the table and was presented with a large plate boasting bacon, eggs and hash brown.
"This looks delicious."
"There's some toast to go along with it. How do you take your coffee?"
"I'm....I'm not too sure."
"You English really are a nation of tea drinkers, aren't you?"

"I suppose so. But with coffee I'm happy with whatever you recommend."

"Ok well, this has some milk in it and just a little sugar. If you want it sweeter just let me know."

Sophia reached over to place the hot mug down on the table, getting close enough for Robert to smell her perfume; he was momentarily transfixed as the sweet smell filled his nostrils.

"Well, aren't you going to try it?"

"Oh, sorry......yes of course."

The question had re-gathered Robert's attention and he took a large sip.

"Mmmm, very nice indeed," feigned Robert.

"You see, tea isn't everything after al.,"

Robert gave a nod of approval and started eating his food. And as Sophia sat down opposite him Robert couldn't help but think that the meal was almost perfect, the only thing missing being a cup of tea.

"So what brings you here?"

"I thought you did, I was knocked out."

"No I don't mean here," she said as she rolled her eyes, "I mean *here*."

Robert knew what she had meant but didn't want to give away anything about his new job.

"I'm here to do some consultancy work."

"Sounds important."

"It's not; to be honest I'm sure you'd find it very dull."

"Is that a fact?"

"Yes."

"And do you think the cause that you are working for is dull?" asked Sophia as she stared at him, her dark eyes fixed firmly upon his.

"How do you know what work I'm involved in?"

"Well firstly I hear that a great English lawyer is going to help our legal team, then I meet an Englishman, find his satchel which is full of notes and legal documents so it's not too hard to figure out. What I'm wondering is why you brought your dad with you."

Robert sighed heavily,

"I didn't bring him.......he brought me."

"I don't understand."

Robert considered trying to make up a credible story but something about Sophia made him feel he could trust her.

"I'm not the great English lawyer you're talking about, my father is......or more accurately, was."

Sophia stared at him in disbelief.

"That drunk man who attacked you is the lawyer? He was about to smash a bottle over your head! I have to let Jim know."

"No you can't!" exclaimed Robert.

"We can't pin our hopes on that man, he's a drunk."

"You don't know what he's been through."

"Well he doesn't know what folks round here have been through either but they don't get drunk and start fights, I've no faith in him."

Robert got up and knelt down beside Sophia, taking her hand in his.

"You don't have to have faith in him; all I'm asking is that you have faith in *me*. I'll be doing all the work and I promise I won't let anyone down."

Sophia turned to face Robert,

"Can you promise, you won't let me down?"

Robert stroked a few loose strands of hair back behind Sophia's ear and gently placed his hand on her cheek.

"I won't let you down," said Robert as he slowly leaned forward and kissed her. Her body rose as she returned his kiss and the pair were locked in a passionate exchange which soon took them from the kitchen to the bedroom.

*****

Charles was crestfallen; he felt sick with shame. Tears filled his eyes as he stared into the mirror. He knew he had to make amends as soon as possible but couldn't remember how they had parted or where his son was now. He knocked on Robert's door and stepped into the room to find the bed still immaculately made. A quick scan of the living room indicated two things; firstly that Robert wasn't there and secondly that Charles had continued drinking after he came home yesterday, the remnants of a bottle of bourbon serving as evidence of yesterday's drinking crime scene. The sight of the bottle made Charles feel ill and he clumsily raced to the bathroom, making it just before he vomited. Every heave caused a lot of pain as it was accompanied by an agonising contraction once again of stomach muscles.

Charles lifted some water to his mouth and felt it cool the whole way down into his stomach. He felt weak as he stood in the bathroom, splashing some water over his face. He then thought he heard a noise coming from the front door.

"Robert?"

There was no reply.

"Robert is that you? I'm so sorry."

Still no reply.

Charles decided he must've been hearing things and continued freshening up in the bathroom. However he soon heard the definite sound of footsteps in the hall and was certain that Robert was in the house.

"Robert? Thank goodness you're back!" shouted Charles, still in the bathroom frantically drying his face.

"Listen son, I know you must be very angry and you've every right to be. I want you to know that things are going to change around here."

Still no reply.

"What's more, I'm going to change," said Charles as he burst out of the bathroom, only to find the figure standing in his hallway was not Robert.

"What are you doing here?"

"Funny, I was about to ask you the same question," replied the stranger who nodded to another figure standing behind Charles.

Charles had not been aware of the second person and turned around but was struck violently on the back of the head, a blow that knocked him unconscious.

*****

The sound of a running shower gently woke Robert from a most relaxing and peaceful sleep. He laid spread out, naked, in the centre of the double bed.

"What time is it?" he shouted after a few minutes.

"It's just after four," came the reply from the bathroom, Sophia straining to make her voice heard above the sound of the rickety old shower.

Robert knew he had to get back soon and set about dressing himself, however his clothes were scattered through the house in a trail from the kitchen to the bedroom. Retracing his steps he eventually retriev
ed all missing items. He was sat on the bed tying his shoes when Sophia came into the room wrapped in a white towel, her long wet hair sleeked back and her dark skin appearing even more smooth and supple.

"You planning on running off?" she said.

"Yeah I best be going. I've a lot of work to do."

Sophia looked disappointed.

"Ok, but please remember what you promised me."

Robert got up and placed his hands around Sophia's waist, holding her damp body close to his.

"I won't forget. Can I see you again?"

"Maybe," she playfully replied.

"Maybe?"

"Yes, it's a small town. You never know who you might bump into."

"Well I'm hoping I bump into you again."

"I'm hoping so too," replied Sophia and the pair kissed for a final time before Robert left.

The walk home in the soaring heat should've been exhausting but Robert was walking on air as he made the long journey back on foot. He felt so good in fact he had forgotten about Charles' behaviour the day before. Arriving home Robert breezed up the front steps to find the front door wide open, suddenly he couldn't help but let thoughts of the day before creep back into his mind. Robert took a deep breath and stepped inside.

Something wasn't right. Pictures lay strewn across the floor. Robert tip-toed past them to find the kitchen a mess of broken plates, smashed glasses and upturned chairs. He had never known Charles to be so destructive but catching his reflection in one of the glass-fronted cabinets reminded him of his father's destructive tendencies yesterday.

"Father, are you here?"

Robert knew that Charles would be nursing a major hangover and thus would be unlikely to venture outside today if at all possible.

Robert then heard a faint groan coming from the bathroom. He stormed off down the hall and discovered the prone figure of Charles lying face down in the doorway. He was surrounded by a pool of blood which emanated from a cut just above his ear. He had been there for some time; the blood now a morose ruby shade, rather than fresh crimson.

"Charles, Charles, wake up," shouted Robert frantically. He rolled his father over to reveal a side of his face caked in dried blood. He could see that Charles was still breathing but besides that displayed little sign of life. Robert propped his father up, resting his head in his lap. He peeled back both eyelids to find each eye looking upwards vacantly. Robert shouted and slapped him on either cheek but to no avail. Then when it seemed hope was fading Charles let out a feeble whimper. Robert immediately started slapping his cheeks again and Charles replied with an almighty groan. He was conscious but the pain meant he wasn't grateful to be.

"Thank God," exclaimed Robert, whose emotions quickly changed to anger.

"Just what the hell did you do to yourself?"

Before Charles could reply he felt his stomach tighten and he raced over to the toilet to vomit.

"Look Charles, this can't go on!"

"I didn't do this Robert. "

There's always an excuse isn't there? Some reason why nothing is your fault! Well I've got news for you, if you don't get a grip you're going to kill yourself. Look at you now, who knows what would've happened if I hadn't arrived."

"Robert, please, you don't....."

"I don't what? Don't deserve to talk to you like this? Don't know how hard it's been since mum died? Believe me I know, I know every single day, but you have to be strong, drinking isn't going to take away the pain!"

"Robert listen!" exclaimed Charles, "You don't understand, I didn't do this."

"What do you mean?"

"Someone was here."

The sentence struck fear into the heart of Robert.

"I woke up and heard a noise. I thought it was you so I went out to apologise for yesterday, but there was a stranger stood there. He spoke to me then someone else hit me on the back of the head. The next thing I know, you're here."

"Are you sure?"

"Yes, 100% sure."

"You said he spoke to you, what did he say?"

"He asked me what I was doing here, but before I could reply his partner walloped me."

Robert took a deep breath.

"And what did he look like?"

"I'm not totally sure, but I think he was quite tall. Yes, he was definitely tall, with blonde hair. I can't believe anyone would do this, especially someone as young as him.

The sick feeling returned to Robert's stomach.

Chapter Eleven

The evening was uncomfortably warm as Robert returned home. His skin had become used to the strong sun and was turning olive. He nodded to a man sat parked in a nearby car and then went inside.

"I see they're still looking out for you?"

"What do you mean?" replied Charles, not looking away from the newspaper he was reading.

"I mean the man outside. He must be baking in this heat."

Charles still didn't lift his gaze from the paper.

"It's for our own good Robert. After all, we won't be much help to the Dallas County Voters if we aren't safe in our own home."

Robert knew Charles had a point but felt guilty that someone had to endure the soaring temperature just to protect them. He also resented the fact that Charles referred to 'we' not being able to help.

"Well, as you're feeling so secure in your home, I trust you got the notes prepared on that new legislation like you said you were going to?"

Charles finally lifted his head from the paper.

"Well, Robert, the thing is......."

"I knew it," sighed Robert.

"Look, it's not like this is important. Besides, the longer we draw out our work, the more we get paid. Seeing as we're living under threat I think that's the least we can expect by way of compensation."

"That's completely ridiculous," fumed Robert.

"How do you mean?"

"Firstly, this *is* important work we're doing, or meant to be doing. Secondly, the DCVL is spending a lot of money; they don't have much so my thinking is they'll want to see a return on their investment. Besides, do you not feel bad about getting paid for doing very little?"

Charles wasn't moved by Robert's question. He still couldn't fathom why Robert felt so strongly about their work. He had never seen him show an interest in civil rights before but during the last few days Robert seemed incredibly committed to the cause.

"Look, just start pulling your weight or we'll both be finished."

"Okay. I'll make a start on reviewing the new legislation tomorrow," said Charles, returning to his paper.

"You do that. Right now I've a meeting organised with one of the locals that was refused access to register to vote."

"You're heading back out?"

"Yes, they weren't able to meet me at our office so I said I'd visit them after work."

"Robert I wish you had told me, I could have got Jim to organise a car for your safety. Hold on and I'll call him now."

"It's fine. I feel bad enough they've had to assign us a security guard outside, I don't want a personal chauffeur too. Besides, Jim will be wondering why you wouldn't be going to speak with them."

Robert immediately regretted his last comment.

"In that case I'll come with you. Wait two seconds and I'll get a car to pick us up."

"No, no, don't be silly," replied Charles, wrecking his brain for some inspiration;

"It's going to be a very brief meeting.....to be honest I've gathered most of the information pertaining to the case already. I just thought I should personally speak with the individual but the chances are it will be a waste of time. Besides, the DCVL will want you working on the most important issues, rather than a minor detail such as this meeting."

Robert studied Charles's expression as he processed this information. He had deliberately played to Charles's weakness, his vanity, and was hoping that his father would take the bait.

"Very well, I'll stay here to concentrate on the legislation," said Charles, content that Robert had recognised his importance.

"But please be careful and come back as soon as you can."

"I will," said Robert as he breathed a sigh of relief and, gathering his bag, he left the house.

*****

Recent events had made Robert nervous as he walked to Sophia's house. He decided to take a longer route and stopped every so often to make sure he wasn't being followed. The sun had almost set as he approached her house; the cool twilight finally offered some respite from the unforgiving heat of earlier that day. One final check satisfied Robert that he was being paranoid and he rapped the front door. Sophia emerged a few seconds later as she opened the door. A glass porch still separated the pair and she smiled as she opened it, greeting Robert with a passionate kiss as she did so.

"My, you're certainly happy to see me."

Robert decided not to explain that the walk there had filled him with a sense of nervous energy.

"What can I say, it seems like a lifetime since I last saw you," replied Robert, slightly embarrassed by his comment, although it was music to Sophia's ears.

"Yeah, I've missed you too."

It had been a long time since anyone had referred to Robert in such a pleasant way; he liked it.

"How have things been?"

"Fine, I guess. I've been working a lot of night shifts at the hospital but I'm off tomorrow. How is your work going? Is your dad helping much?"

There was an implied tone to the question which Robert did well to ignore.

"It's been good. We've made some really significant progress. In fact, as we speak my father is going through some important legislation with a fine tooth comb."

Sophia looked at him quizzically;

"Really?"

"Absolutely," Robert could feel his cheeks burning.

"That's good. But hey, you didn't come here to talk about work. Come on in, dinner will be ready in a few minutes."

"Thank you," replied Robert, happy for the reprieve from lying, "would it be alright if I used your bathroom?"

"Of course, you know where it is?"

"I remember," said Robert with a warm smile.

    Robert was keen to have a look round Sophia's house. He hadn't seen much of it apart from the bedroom and kitchen and found her living situation intriguing. The sound of chopping confirmed Sophia was in the kitchen so, upon leaving the bathroom, he headed further down the hall. The first door he opened was for a closet containing an ironing board, a mop and some towels. He closed the door softly but the old handle noisily clicked back into place. The sound reverberated down the hall and Robert turned anxiously and froze, listening to determine if Sophia had heard. After a few breathless seconds he heard Sophia was still in the kitchen so set about continuing. Robert gingerly clasped the handle of another door and after softly pushing it down he lightly stepped into the darkened room. He ran his fingers across the wall and found a light-switch. The room, now illuminated, contained a large, perfectly-made bed in the centre, flanked by two bedside tables. Each was decorated with a selection of framed pictures, with a clock on one side and an elegant ivory comb on the other. Robert stepped across the room and lifted one

of the pictures. It was from some time ago but he recognised the young girl in the picture as Sophia. She was sitting on a woman's lap and a man was standing behind them, with his arm on the woman's shoulder. Robert presumed these were her parents as all three looked very happy. As he studied the expression on each of their faces a series of painful memories came creeping back. He had tried not to think about his mother but this grainy picture circumvented his self-imposed memory block.
"What are you doing?"
The angry tone snapped Robert out of his painful daze and he turned round to find Sophia stood in the doorway.
"I'm sorry, I......."
"You what? Thought you'd have a sneak around my place?"
"No, I....I'm sorry, I got confused. I thought this room was the bathroom," Robert realised how ridiculous that sounded;
"And then, when I turned on the light I saw a picture of you so, I thought I would have a look. I didn't mean to......"
Robert was interrupted by Sophia who marched forward and ripped the picture out of his hand.
"I didn't mean to upset you."
Sophia had her back to him as she slowly placed the picture back on the table.
Robert placed a hand around her waist.
"I'm sorry, I really didn't........"
"That's okay," said Sophia, exhaling loudly.
"I know you didn't mean any harm. It's just, I haven't been in this room for a long time."
"Why not?" asked Robert softly.
"I don't come into this room because it's full of things like this," she said, pointing to the picture.
"The photographs, the jewellery, the small mementos, it's a room full of sad memories. I just haven't been able to bring myself to do something about it."
Robert watched in silence as he studied the room, each detail a fragment from a former, happier life.
"Can I ask how they died?"
Sophia turned round, tears filling her big brown eyes as she stared directly into his.
"I'd rather not talk about it."
"That's okay," said Robert, gently rubbing her back.
"I really didn't mean to upset you."

Sophia wiped a tear from her eye, determined to not let Robert see her being weak anymore.

"It's okay hun.........you're quite the dinner date aren't you, coming over and getting a girl all upset?"

Sophia tried to fake a smile but Robert could see she was still hurting.

"I'm sorry. How can I make it up to you?"

"You can start by pouring two glasses of wine."

"Will do chef," replied Robert, following Sophia out of the room.

Suddenly he did not feel so alone in the world of family grief.

*****

"Is he in there?" said a shrill voice.

Errol hadn't been aware of anyone behind him and the shock made him jump.

"Fucking hell, how are you meant to keep lookout if you don't see someone coming from behind you?"

Errol's pulse was racing as he tried to identify the shadowy figure now crouching beside him. It was dark in the undergrowth and Errol's eyes had been studying the house through a pair of binoculars, with these now removed his vision was struggling to adjust to the darkness.

"You not hear me? I asked if he's in there?" said the unidentified figure, angrily.

"Yeah, he's inside alright."

"Good, cause Carter will be here soon. We're on duty tonight."

Errol raised the binoculars again. The mention of Carter meant two things; firstly, that the person next to him was almost definitely Williams and secondly, someone was going to get hurt.

"Hold on, he's not alone," said Errol.

"You telling me that nigger-lover has a bitch round?"

"No. I mean he's being watched by someone else besides us. Here, take a look."

Errol reached the binoculars to who he now recognised to be Williams. He was wearing jeans, a dark shirt and a black hat which hid his blonde locks.

Williams took a look at the man positioned down the street a bit.

"I see what you mean. Looks like we might get two for the price of one," said Williams, ominously.

"What time is Carter gonna be here?"

"He's already here."

The response served to immediately speed Errol's heart-rate again.

"What do you mean, he's already here?"

"He told me he'd be watching from nightfall. You know what he's like; he'll want to get an idea of the house."

Errol was panicking. He knew Carter would have been watching *him* as well as the house. For all he knew he was being watched right now; the thought sent a shiver down Errol's spine.

"Did you not tell him bout the house? We....we got a pretty good idea of the layout from when we were here before, remember?"

"Don't worry big E. I told him all that we saw from the last time. I also made sure and told him that it was you who cracked the old bastard over the head. I tell you something, he was impressed with you."

"Really, he was impressed?"

"Yeah, dead impressed."

Errol felt his whole body relax.

"He's probably checking out the surrounding area, you know, the best way to escape should something go wrong."

From what Errol had heard, not much went wrong when Carter was involved. And if it did, the plan of escape usually involved bloodshed.

"Should we try and find him?"

"Don't be fucking stupid E. You were ordered to keep watch so that is exactly what you'll do. I'll find him and come back here. Now keep your eyes open, this is an important one tonight."

With that Williams left, crawling face down back over the verge he had first come through before disappearing into the night. And as Errol surveyed the house once again he couldn't shift the unnerving feeling of being watched.

*****

"That was delicious," said Robert as he surrendered his knife and fork to the centre of the empty plate.

"Would you like some more?"

"Sophia I couldn't eat another bite."

Robert contentedly rubbed his stomach as Sophia lifted his plate from the table.

"Let me do that."

"Don't be silly, you're my guest."

Robert stood up and forcibly removed the plate from Sophia's grasp;

"It's the least I can do. Now leave the tidying up to me. Just you relax and have some more wine."

"Oh very well....if you insist."

Robert refilled Sophia's glass and ushered her into taking a soft seat in the living room;

"I'll join you in a few minutes, as soon as I'm done."

With that Robert headed back to the kitchen. He ran the hot tap and refilled his wine glass as he waited for the sink to fill. After scraping the remains of the meal into the bin he placed the plates and saucepans into the sink. He then lifted a dishcloth and set about cleaning the first plate but the water was piping hot. In his haste Robert had forgotten to run the cold tap. After a couple of failed attempts at bearing the heat Robert accepted defeat and decided that he would come back and finish the dishes after the water had cooled down.

"My, that was quick," exclaimed Sophia as Robert re-entered the room.

"Well, I'm not finished yet but I thought it would be best to let the dishes seep for a while."

Robert smiled warmly as he sat down beside Sophia on the large sofa. She returned the smile, her previously pristine white teeth now stained by red wine. And as he lifted his glass to his mouth to take a large glug Robert caught Sophia staring at him. Perhaps it was the abundance of wine, or the realisation that they had both lost loved ones but Robert had not felt this close to anyone in a long time.

"You look beautiful," said Robert.

"You're drunk."

"I'm serious," exclaimed Robert, although he did feel a bit drunk.

"You shouldn't say things like that."

"I shouldn't tell a beautiful woman that she looks beautiful?"

"No, you just shouldn't tell me."

Robert placed his hand upon Sophia's neck and pulled her softly towards him to kiss her. He had never wanted anything more in his life.

"Sophia, you are the most beautiful woman I have ever met."

As she stared at him Robert was a mixture of excitement and anticipation. Eventually she leaned forward and kissed him, softly at first but becoming more frantic as the passion increased with each exchange. Drunken desire took over as Robert positioned his hands under her midriff and in one fluent motion pulled her on top of him. As she straddled him Robert frantically undid the buttons in her blouse. Upon opening the final one Sophia arched her back and Robert leaned forward, kissing her cleavage as she pulled his head forward into her breasts. Sophia moaned with pleasure as Robert's hands caressed her chest. She then sat forward and determinedly pulled his shirt over the top of his head. With Sophia's legs still wrapped around his waist Robert rose to his feet and placed her down on the sofa. He then leaned over her and, after the pair removed the remainder of each other's clothes, they made love.

*****

The news that Carter was in the vicinity had sharpened Errol's senses. He did not want to get caught off guard again, especially not by Carter. Errol looked at his watch, it had been almost two hours since Williams had left and the temperature had dropped considerably. Errol could now see his breath in the cool night air but was determined not to leave his post. Instead he sat upright and pulled his legs into his chest to maximise his body heat. 'Next time I'll bring a dark coat,' he thought to himself.

He was snapped back to attention by a cracking nearby. It sounded like a twig breaking or an animal rustling in the bushes. Errol began to get nervous and fumbled inside his chest pocket to reach for his knife. He had never had to use the knife but was instructed to always carry a weapon in case of emergency. As the sound drew closer he wasn't sure he would be able to do so.
"Psstt, big E," said a familiar voice.
"I'm here Williams," said Errol, releasing the knife from his grasp and placing it carefully back inside his pocket.
"No names!" said another person in a commanding manner.
The voices came from behind Errol. He couldn't see Williams or the other person from his vantage point and so crawled back out of the ditch into the field which ran directly behind his lookout spot. There along the tree line, almost invisible to the eye, stood Williams and another figure Errol presumed to be Carter. He was tall and broad, even his stance was menacing.
"The big man's right," said Williams, "we're not using names from now on so let's get this out of the way now. Errol this is Carter."
Errol stepped forward and stretched out a hand. Carter stood motionless for a few seconds before abrasively shaking Errol's hand in reply. He didn't speak and as he shook Errol's hand he stared at him with an agitated expression. His furrowed brow

was beset with deep-set wrinkles and his face was marked with a large scar, running from above his left eye down to his cheek. This precluded the left eye from opening fully but Errol was too nervous to look for more than a split second.

"Right, we're moving," said Williams as Carter released his clamp-like grip.

"I take it he's still inside big E?"

"Yeah he's there alright, security's still watching the place a few doors down."

"Do you know if the son is inside?" asked Carter gruffly.

Errol realised immediately this was a test;

"He left the house a few hours ago; word is he's shacked up with some nigger over on the far side of town so I don't think we'll see him again tonight."

Carter nodded by way of approval, both at the news that he was out of the house and that Errol had been sharp enough to correctly surmise the situation.

"How do you want to handle this C?"

Errol considered Williams' use of first letters almost as obvious as the name itself but he wasn't going to go against Carter's expressed orders.

"First we got to bag the lookout,"

"OK, do you want me to take care of him?"

"No, I think *big E* is the man for the job."

Carter stared directly at Errol, trying to sense a reaction. Errol was careful not to flinch or show weakness. Inside he was terrified but once again he knew he was being tested; he didn't want to fail Carter.

"You sure?" asked Williams, disappointed he was not getting the opportunity to impress Carter.

"Certain. After all, you told me big E here knocked the fucker out with just one hit, clean as a whistle."

Carter imitated swinging a bat as he spoke, finishing with the pretend bat pointed directly at Errol.

"You got a weapon okay?"

Williams' question made what Errol was being asked to do become a stark reality.

"I got a knife," he replied timidly.

"See, he's ready. He's even got his own knife," said Carter sarcastically, enjoying his position of authority over the pair.

Errol swallowed hard and cleared his throat,

"How'd you want me to do this?"

"What we need you to do is to take him out with minimal fuss. We don't want anything drawing attention to you, or to us."

Errol nodded. His stomach was a pit of nerves but he was trying not to let this show.

"Ok, do you want me to give you a signal when the coast is clear?"

"No, we'll be watching," said Carter.

"Understood," replied Errol and, after drawing a deep breath, he headed off along the tree-line of the field, a path that would lead him to within 50 yards of the house.

"Hold on a second E," said a voice from behind Errol.

It was Carter standing with a cigarette in his mouth and a bat in his hand. The sight shocked Errol and he was scared and confused.

"Have you ever killed someone before?"

"Excuse me?"

Carter removed the cigarette,

"I said, have you ever killed a man?"

"No, no I haven't," replied Errol, not enjoying the feeling of being ridiculed.

Carter stared at him for a few seconds as he inhaled, trying to get a gauge on Errol's emotional state. Eventually he spoke;

"Well here, take this bat instead."

"You sure?"

"Yeah I'm sure. To kill someone you gotta have ice in your veins, especially if you plan killing them with a knife. I don't want to risk this cause of you freezing on us. Just make sure you knock him out cold. Don't let the fucker know we're coming."

With that Carter turned and walked back to where Williams was waiting. For a second Errol felt slightly insulted but this quickly turned to massive relief as he realised he was no longer being asked to kill. It may have seemed a small reprieve but Errol was extremely grateful for it.

*****

Robert felt calm; a sensation he had not felt for a very long time. As he lay naked beside Sophia he felt her body rise and fall with each inhalation and exhalation. Beads of sweet trickled down her back as she peacefully dozed. Robert lay behind her, a protective arm placed across her shoulder. It felt good to have someone to protect.

When Sophia woke she opened her eyes to find Robert already awake. He was stroking her hair softly.

"How long was I asleep for?"

"About twenty minutes."

Sophia realised she was naked and began to feel self-conscious.

"I'm going to freshen up, can I get you anything?"

"How about you bring what's left of that bottle of wine?"

"Sounds good," said Sophia, giving Robert a kiss as she got up from the couch. Robert could see through the window that it was still dark outside. He pulled his trousers back on and sat up. As he gazed out the window his thoughts began to wonder; he was becoming convinced that someone special had entered his life but felt a sense of sorrow for the person who had left. Charles was alone tonight, as he had been ever since his mother's passing.

"What's on your mind?"

Robert had been so deep in concentration he had not noticed her coming back into the room. The question broke his trance and he looked up to find Sophia stood wrapped in a dressing gown, a bottle of wine in her hand.

"I was just thinking about someone."

"Someone from back home?"

"Yes, well no, actually......but sort of."

"Sounds complicated. Who is she, a girlfriend?"

"No. I was thinking about my mother."

"Did she not come here?"

"No, she died years ago."

"Oh, I am sorry Robert."

"It's fine. I wasn't thinking about her. It was more how my father hasn't been able to come to terms with losing her."

"Has he always struggled to accept her death?"

"I think so........I can't be sure. We fell out years ago. In fact her illness was the only thing that brought us together. I know he still harbours a lot of resentment and anger over losing her, and over how things turned out."

"Why did you fall out?"

Robert sighed heavily, turning his gaze from Sophia.

"I was young, just out of University and wanted to spread my wings. You know, live a little. Well, unknown to me he had arranged for me to serve as an apprentice in a renowned London firm. I told him I didn't want to be tied down, that I wanted to make my own way and not rely on him doing favours for me. Looking back now I was naive. This angered him and a bitter argument ensued wherein I told him I didn't want to live his life. It escalated further, things were said on both sides that we couldn't take back. Eventually culminating in the point where he said I had always been a disappointment as a son."

"Oh my God, that's horrible."

"I know. The thing is that I had always wanted to follow in his footsteps but not because of what favours he could do for me. He never understood that, but the only thing I wanted to do was make him proud."

"So what happened?"

That same day I packed my things and left. Mum was heartbroken but I told her I wasn't staying another day in the same house as him. Neither of us would back down so I walked out and didn't return until she was admitted into hospital. And now I have him to thank for ending my legal career back home. But still I can't help but feel sorry for him."

He turned and looked at Sophia, "I guess what I'm saying is that I've met someone special and he's alone. It must be hard and I don't think I've helped much."

"I'm sure you have Robert," offered Sophia.

"The thing is, he's never properly grieved for her. He drinks to ease the pain but it doesn't take it away, it just quells the fire for a while but it's always there, just waiting to ignite again."

"And that explains why he was roughing you up outside the bar?"

"Exactly, the mere mention of her name is enough to make him explode."

"I know what you mean. It can be hard to come to terms with losing someone so close."

The phrase hung in the air before the realisation dawned on Robert. How could he have forgotten what he'd discovered only hours earlier that evening? He decided not be the first to break the silence. Sophia sensed his unease;

"It's okay Robert, you don't have to feel bad."

"I'm an idiot. What can I say, I'm sorry."

"There's no need to apologise. You were talking about how you feel and besides, I never explained my situation."

"I know, but I should've been more thoughtful, more aware."

Sophia placed her slender hand over his to silence him.

"No Robert, I should've been more open. If I had you would understand why your work means so much to me."

Robert looked on, intently.

"You can tell me now."

"Ok," said Sophia, drawing a deep breath.

"My father, the person you saw in the picture, was a great man. He believed strongly in civil liberty and justice. He was also very brave and wasn't afraid of anybody."

Robert could see tears starting to form in Sophia's big brown eyes.

"He was one of the principal organisers of the civil rights movement here, with a passion and belief that I could only dream about emulating. He didn't see things, people, as being one thing or another. He just saw people as human beings and each entitled to the same rights and freedoms. This made him a target.

Sophia looked out the door.

"I still remember the look on his face that night. He had been out at a rally, trying to register people to vote in one of the churches in the east side of town. A crowd of men broke into our house. I was only little and in their white sheets and hoods, they looked like ghosts. I was terrified, so was my mother. They held me and my mom in the house while they waited for him to come back. When he did they gave him the choice, either leave town tonight or they would kill his family."

Sophia swallowed hard as a tear ran down her cheek.

"He said.......he said he would leave. I remember.....I remember being so scared. One of the men had a knife to mom's throat. They said they'd let her go. They said they'd let us all go."

Tears ran freely down Sophia's cheek.

"Then the man cut her throat. She hadn't done anything, he was pure evil. My dad couldn't control himself and he lashed out. He caught the first man with a punch to the head and for a while they couldn't contain him, he was like a wild animal. He dived at the man who had killed her and wrestled the knife out of his hand, slicing the man's face. But then I heard a gunshot and my father dropped to the floor. I can still see his eyes as he fell; they were completely hollow and bereft of life, like his spirit had already gone."

"Sophia, I had no idea."

Sophia's breathing eventually began to calm.

"And that's the sight I keep seeing at night, my father's empty eyes. I never dream about the good moments, it's always those dead eyes. They've haunted me since I first saw them; they haunt me still."

*****

Errol stood motionless, like a rabbit caught in headlights. He had followed the tree line as far as he could but the last stage of his journey would be completed without this cover. From his position he could see the feint light of a cigarette glowing brighter with each inhalation. Errol's vain hope that the personal security guard had fallen asleep was shattered. For a second he looked back to where Carter and Williams had been, hoping that they might try and signal him to come back. However he realised that going back to face Carter without having attempted his task was more daunting than the task itself.

The problem was getting close enough to the car to strike, without the bat being seen. Errol thought about leaving the bat but stabbing someone was a step further than he was prepared to go. Instead he came up with a plan which seemed to get him close up to the guard, what happened next would be less certain.

Errol reached into his pocket and pulled out his knife; the blade flashing momentarily as it caught the moonlight. He cut off his left sleeve, leaving only a ragged, loose piece of material to cover his upper left arm. Next was the hard part. Errol took a deep breath and clenched his teeth before running the sharp blade along his forearm. The incision was long, and deeper than Errol had intended. Bright red blood started seeping from the wound. Undeterred, Errol stood up straight and released his belt. He then lifted the bat and placed it inside his trouser leg, with the handle perched just above the top of his belt. Finally he tightened the belt again to hold the bat in place and pulled his top down to cover the protruding end of the handle.

'This is going to work' he thought to himself.

Errol stepped out from the relative security of the cover and into the open space. He paced gingerly up the centre of the road, taking small steps to avoid the bat being visible. As he crept forward he held his forearm tight. It was bleeding heavily and Errol could feel the arm throbbing as he squeezed harder, trying to limit the blood loss. With his right hand now covered in the claret fluid he ran his hand across his face as a soldier would for camouflage, the difference was Errol wanted to be seen.

The presence of the bat gave Errol a seemingly natural limp and he was now within 15 yards of the parked car, approaching it from behind. He continued to walk down the centre of the road and kept his eyes looking down at the ground, he knew he was being watched by both parties now.

"Help......help," he whimpered softly as he crept to within five yards of the car.

His heart began to race as he heard the door open. Errol continued to stare downwards and limp forward but he could tell by the sound of footsteps that the man was stood directly in his path.

"Shit, what happened to you son?"

Errol pretended to be surprised by the question and looked up to find a tall burly figure staring at him. The size and stature of the man made him seem imposing but he looked at Errol with concern in his eyes.

"Oh, help me, sir. I.....I got jumped a while back. They took my money and cut me, real bad."

"How comes you walking here?"

Errol hadn't been expecting any questions.

"Well I don't have my money so can't call home, or the police, and I don't think folks would let me into their house if I came a knocking in the middle of the night looking like I do. I ain't seen any houses with lights on yet anyways. Can you please help me sir?"

"Sure, where did they cut you boy?"

"They cut me on the arm, they also cut my head I reckon."

The man stepped forward to inspect the extent of the cut to the head. Errol grimaced slightly; he knew it was a mistake to say his head had been cut and one that may force his hand. With the man close and now distracted by examining his head Errol slowly reached his hand down to his hip and grasped the handle of the bat. Adrenaline was coursing through his veins as he counted himself down, three, two, one....

"Son I can't see any cuts to your head, are you sure..."

Like a swordsman drawing his blade Errol swiftly removed the bat from his trouser leg and in one fluent movement swung it at the man's head. However, the close proximity meant that Errol couldn't deliver a powerful strike and the man raised his forearm to partially deflect the blow. Panicking, Errol tried to swing again but the man stepped forward and grabbed the end of the bat. As the pair wrestled for possession it was obvious Errol was weaker than his opponent and with a strong shrug Errol was dispossessed.

"Boy, I'm gonna enjoy this," said the man as he paced forward, bat in hand.

Errol had been thrown up against the side of the car as a result of the grapple. He swallowed hard as he realised he had no chance of escape. He tensed himself as the man drew the bat back and Errol closed his eyes, awaiting the impending doom but the sound of a shotgun firing bellowed across the night. Shocked, he opened his eyes to see the man falling to the ground. Fear then took Errol prisoner as he lay on the ground, frozen.

"Get the fuck out of here!" came a cry from down the street. Errol snapped back to life and darted down the road faster than he had ever ran before. He made it to the tree line after a matter of seconds but Carter and Williams had not stopped there.

Errol's lungs were burning and his legs weak as the adrenalin rush began to fade but he kept running, scared of what he was running from, and fearful of what he was now running towards.

Chapter Twelve

Robert's world was about to implode. The early morning journey home had once again left him feeling of calm but this would evaporate in the commotion that awaited him.

From a distance Robert could see something was amiss; the police cars and flashing lights a sickening indication of trouble. He broke into a sprint as he neared the house, desperately trying not to allow any thoughts to enter his head as he feared what they might be. Robert bounded up the stairs and through the front door to find the house full of people, many of whom he had not seen before.

"What's happened?"

"There was an incident last night," replied one of the strangers.

"What do you mean, incident? Is my father okay?"

A sorrowful Jim appeared in the hallway.

"Jim, Jim, what's happened? Is something wrong with my father?"

"There was a shooting last night Robert."

"Fucking hell, is he dead? Is my dad dead? Robert put his head in his hands.

"No Robert, you're father is fine. It was his personal security guard that was shot. He.......he was shot early this morning.........he's dead, Robert."

As tears began to swell in Jim's eyes Robert knew that the man meant something special to him. However Robert was relieved that Charles was still alive at this man's expense; he also hated himself for that.

As Robert continued down the hall into the kitchen he saw Charles being interviewed by two white police officers sat at the table. He looked visibly shaken by the incident; the glass of golden brown liquid next to him was another indication that the event had rocked him. Robert watched on as Charles answered their questions for a further few minutes then, as the officers stepped away, Charles caught sight of Robert and beckoned him over.

"Thank God you're alright."

Charles's hand was shaking as he lifted the glass to his mouth. He took a large gulp and sat the glass back down noisily on the table.

"I don't think that's a good idea right now," offered Robert.

"Not a good idea?"

Robert saw the anger flashing in Charles's eyes.

"Someone tried to kill me last night. They came here to get me, and kill me, and you're going to begrudge me having a drink to try and calm myself!"

Charles's voice grew louder, so much so that some people in the room were beginning to stare.

"Okay, okay, calm down," replied Robert through gritted teeth, trying to quell the underlying anger and not make a scene.

"All I meant was that Jim is here and it might not look too good if you're having a few drinks."

"Jim's paying no attention to me. Besides, he could have mentioned before I came that there would be a risk of death involved in the work. The bastard kept that small detail very quiet."

"That's enough," barked Robert, in a louder tone than he had intended. He quickly re-gathered his composure.

"Look, Jim is a mess right now because one of his friends is dead. And he died protecting you, so I don't think you should cause him any stress."

"Suppose you're right," conceded Charles as he slumped back into his chair, "doesn't matter anyway, there's no way we're continuing to work here."

"You're going to quit?"

"Absolutely. How can we be expected to work under these conditions? It's not safe son."

"We.....we...can't be intimidated. We have to keep going."

Charles stared at Robert inquisitively.

"Why do *we* have to keep going? This isn't our cause to fight."

"But I know that we can make a difference, if we just keep......"

"We're not going to keep doing anything here!" snapped Charles, cutting off Robert's argument.

"Look," replied Robert, "it's not like we have a lot of options right now. We can't go back home and we don't have enough money to support us for any length of time while we try to find a new employer."

"That won't be a problem. My reputation is such that......"

"You're reputation is finished!"

This time it was Robert who cut Charles off.

"It was Hector who got you this job, he vouched for your good character and ability but that was based on what you did *before*. But everyone back home and practically everyone who's anyone over here would not touch you from a mile off."

Charles looked on in disbelief.

"Hector told me as much. In fact he made me promise to take on the main responsibility wherever possible. The Voters League was so desperate that they were the only one's willing to take a chance on you but even still he knew he was

76

taking a risk in recommending you. That's why he asked me to keep you in the background as best I could."

After delivering this truthful dagger Robert immediately felt guilty. It had clearly struck a painful chord with Charles. The pair sat silent.

"Look, I'm sorry."

Charles clenched his lower jaw but said nothing. He was staring at the glass in his hand as the emotional demons inside him waged war.

"I'm sorry, I shouldn't have....."

"Get out," said Charles, slowly but sternly.

"Look I shouldn't have....."

"Get out!" exploded Charles, throwing his glass across the room. It smashed loudly, indicating that the anger demon had claimed victory. The sound startled the huddled masses spread throughout the kitchen and beyond but as Robert walked past them on his way out the door he did not offer a single word of explanation. There was nothing left to say.

Chapter Thirteen

Errol was trapped in a nightmare from which he could not wake. There had been few words exchanged when he caught up with Williams and Carter. Through a haze of cigarette smoke Carter had simply instructed them to meet him at seven pm in the back car park of Joe's diner, a dilapidated restaurant on the outskirts of town that was being refurbished. At the time Errol had been relieved to get away from the pair but in reality them, and the night's events, were now permanently etched in his mind.

What remained of the night would not allow Errol to sleep and he felt exhausted and weary as he rode the bus into town. He had spent most of the day in a nearby park, hoping that the vibrancy of life would be enough to distract his mind. It had not done so. A series of thoughts each more terrifying than the last regularly bombarded Errol's conscious, like cruel waves upon a battered seashore.

'What if somebody saw?'

'What if he left some evidence at the scene?'

'What if the man had a family?'

'What about Carter?'

The final two thoughts were the most worrying. At this point he would consider being caught an acceptable prospect, in some way he would be getting what he deserved and this may even act as penitence for his sins. At least it might remove some of the guilt that was crippling him. But the victim certainly did not get what he deserved; the image of his lifeless body appeared constantly in Errol's mind's eye. The sick feeling in the pit of his stomach sank a little deeper each time he recalled how he had tricked the man. Errol tried to tell himself that there was nothing to be gained from replaying the scene; the ending would always be the same.

Then there was Carter. Until last night Errol only knew him by reputation but meeting him in person served to amass all the intimidating, ruthless and frightening rumours into an even more sinister character, one that was now very real. And one whose orders Errol had failed to adequately carry out. He searched desperately for crumbs of comfort, for instance the fact that Carter had given him the bat instead of the knife but he knew he was clutching at straws; the bat was supposed to stop Errol making a mistake but he had done so anyway.

As the bus approached Errol's stop he gingerly rose to his feet. He couldn't be sure but he felt like the other passengers were watching him, somehow aware of what he had done. He stepped off and started down the road towards Joe's. It was still daylight but the temperature had reached its angry peak earlier and was now calming, before eventually stepping aside for darkness to temporarily reign.

Errol had decided it best to arrive early so it was just after six thirty by the time he arrived. He was shocked to find Carter already waiting for him as he walked round the back of the car park. He was in the same pose as the last time Errol saw him and looked every bit as intimidating; his chest pushed forward and shoulder blades back, cigarette in hand and an unwelcoming scowl across his face, emphasised further by his facial scar. Errol could feel himself trembling as he approached.

"Right," offered Carter.

"Hey," replied Errol in as deep a voice as he could manage.

Carter did not look at him as he continued to smoke his cigarette down to the butt, grimacing slightly after the last long inhalation. It seemed like an eternity before someone spoke so Errol decided to break the ice.

"No sign of Williams yet?"

"He ain't coming."

Errol's fear jumped up a notch.

"How come?"

Carter stared at him, upset that anyone would dare question him.

"Can't make it. It's fine though, I spoke to him a while back. I know he's cool."

Errol noticed that Carter placed extra emphasis on the last sentence; he recognised this as being another test.

"That's cool. So what's the plan?"

Again Carter looked at him indignantly.

"The plan is, *big E*, that we make sure you aren't going to crack and cry running to the fucking pigs. So what I'm saying is, are you able to handle what happened last night?"

Errol tried to control his nerves.

"Yeah, I'm fucking cool, you don't need to worry bout me."

Carter stared at him, trying to figure out what was going on inside. Eventually he spoke again.

"Yeah man, that's what I like to hear."

This was a massive weight off Errol's mind and for the first time since the incident he felt himself relax slightly. Carter sparked up another cigarette and this time offered the pack to Errol.

"Nah I'm cool man, I'm still buzzing from last night so don't need any hit right now."

Carter stayed silent but Errol, feeling a sense of relief, found himself unable to stop talking.

"You ever been to this place? Joe's I mean?"

Carter shook his head.

"You should go man, its real good. At least it was before they shut it down. I wonder what time the workmen stop here."

Carter stubbed out his cigarette and turned to Errol.

"Five pm."

"Ah that's cool. Do you work here or how comes you know that?"

"Sometimes," replied Carter as he pulled a handgun from his belt holder. Without hesitation he shot Errol twice in the chest before firing a third and final shot him in the head.

"Sometimes," he repeated.

Errol had failed the test.

Chapter Fourteen

When everyone eventually left the house Charles felt alone, more so than he had done in a long time. Following Robert's outburst he had been desperate for some privacy but now his wish had been granted he was ill at ease in his own company. His glass had been replenished twice but was now nearing empty once again. He got up and poured another large bourbon; he was starting to get a taste for it.

For the past few hours he had been dealing with the police, plus Jim and other concerned figures from the Voters League, but his thoughts had been solely upon Robert's revelation. The magnitude of the outburst hit him hard. He was questioning everything he knew, or thought he knew, about himself. It was not a pleasant experience.

He took a drink of the bourbon to try and derail his thoughts but they remained steadily on track.

'How could Hector have so little faith in him, or be so underhand?'
'How could Robert still be so disrespectful?'

As he mulled over the events of the last day Charles's mind began to succumb to the bourbon. He slowly began to convince himself that Robert had been lying. Part of him knew that this was avoiding the real issue, that being what he'd been doing over the past few years but he was happy to accept this facade. He replayed the scenario over and over in his head and each time became more convinced that Robert had an ulterior motive. After all, Robert had not been there last night. His thoughts then turned to Hector; the only explanation Charles could think of was that Hector was jealous of him. Small fragments of conversations, taken out of context and compiled over a number of years were being recalled by Charles, all pointing out what was now the only scenario, Hector's incredible jealousy and bias towards Robert. Hector knew what had transpired between Charles and Robert years earlier and now wanted Robert to eclipse his father. As he continued to warp his mind with bourbon he descended deeper and deeper into his deluded fantasy, now convinced that he had discovered the truth that had been so obvious all along. Any details which seemed to contradict his theories were simply cast aside as Charles began to build a rage inside.

"They think they can take me for a fool!" he bellowed, as he clumsily made his way from the kitchen to his room, managing not to spill a single drop of his precious bourbon.

"Curse them, curse them all!" he raged as he angrily pulled out his suitcase from below the bed.

He started throwing clothes into the case, not taking time to fold or neatly pack; these were unimportant things, just like the people who had wronged him. With his suitcase full he picked up the phone to call Jim. However, as his mind was currently poisoned by alcohol he didn't realise that Jim would not be at home. The constant ringing tone fuelled Charles's frustration further and he ripped the phone off the wall. "Fuck Jim too," he said to nobody in particular.

Charles realised he needed an alternative form of transport and that would require money. Reaching into his pockets he unearthed a handful of dollar bills and loose change. He found a fifty by the side of his bed before raiding Robert's room, sending books and files flying as he angrily discarded them in his search for cash. He found almost $200 dollars folded inside the Bible in Robert's top drawer which caused him to hesitate. For a split second his conscience tried to interject but the alcohol-induced anger soon put paid to that and he snatched the money with a rebellious "fuck you too."

****

Robert felt ravaged with guilt and it was a feeling that annoyed him. He knew that what he said was the truth but he also knew it would have hit his father hard. Even now, after being embarrassingly ordered out of the house in front of his colleagues he still couldn't bring himself to forget about Charles. Robert had to believe there was some remnants of his former self not beyond being saved. For now though he just needed to be away.

  He arrived at the bus stop just in time to see that it was already leaving. For a second he considered running but with no reason to hurry he decided to let it pass. In fact, rather than wait for the next one he chose to walk instead. After all, there was only one place he was going to go and he was in no rush to get there.

  By now the city was alive with life. Colour, sound and energy were rife in every street that Robert passed on his journey. The sun seemed to be acting as a catalyst for this buzz as it had unshackled itself from an early morning haze to now deliver unbroken sunshine. Robert's throat was dry so he decided to get some water from a corner shop. As he entered the man behind the counter stared at him. Robert picked up a bottle and placed it on the counter as the man continued to silently watch him with a disgruntled look upon his face.

"How much?" asked Robert.

"Two dollars," replied the shopkeeper dryly, not versed in good customer service.

Robert put down the two notes and left without saying a word.

The water was cold on the back of his throat. The wine from the night before and the drama from this morning had left Robert more tired and worn out than he realised. Sophia was working until the early afternoon so Robert decided to kill a few hours reading the paper in the park. This meant that he had to go back into the shop he had just exited. Upon his arrival the shopkeeper seemed to be sporting an even more unfriendly face so Robert decided to change tact.

"Great day today", he said chirpily.

"Um-hum."

"Do you happen to have any of today's papers?"

The man sighed deeply and without speaking pointed to a row of papers and magazines which Robert had already seen.

"Ah yes, very good. I believe I'll go for this one," with that Robert put down a dollar fifty on the counter. Again the man said nothing.

"Have a good day friend," quipped Robert.

As Robert left the shop both men whispered 'asshole' under their breath.

Robert continued down the street a few blocks before crossing the road and entering the park. It contained a full spectrum of people all engaged in different activities. Black and white, young and old, male and female all busy enjoying free time in the open spaces. For a while Robert contemplated just how much this was at odds with the events of the previous night. The joyous scenes in front of him would offer no indication of the city's dark underbelly.

Robert strolled deeper into the park until he found a vacant bench. He sat down and swigged the final remnants of his water before unfolding the paper. The headline concerned a civil rights march which had taken place a few towns over but in the same state. Marchers had been confronted by a gang of protestors and the scene had descended into violence. The article speculated that trouble-makers had travelled to the town specifically but that elements within the march had also been predisposed to violence. The outcome had been brutal, with two marchers receiving gunshot wounds and one protestor suffering a broken leg. Despite recent events Robert remained more intrigued than intimidated by the situation and wanted to understand more fully. He now felt a duty to the people he had met, not just Sophia but also Jim, and especially the man who had given his life. Robert felt bad for not even knowing his name. He also felt that if he was not able to save Charles at least he could still connect his name to something worthwhile; perhaps Charles's legacy would not be a sad one.

The article continued over on page three and as Robert digested the full details he felt his eyes becoming heavier and heavier. Eventually he succumbed to the sleep that both his body and mind so desperately craved.

******

Charles was sweating profusely as he loaded his bag onto the bus. It was a very hot day, not ideal for carrying such a heavy bag. As he sat down he felt a layer of moisture across his entire body. His throat was dry and a swig of bourbon from his hip flask was not the tonic for quenching it but he did so anyway. He grimaced as the hot liquid burned his throat. He realised that an old woman had seen him taking the drink but he didn't care, Charles was leaving and there was nothing anyone could do to stop him. He took another mouthful, deliberately turning his head to make eye contact with the woman as he supped from the flask. He had a long journey to the airport and an even longer journey after that. Soon Charles would also give in to sleep but this was the dark, dreamless slumber of a man that was drowning the painful voices inside.

A sharp jolt snapped Charles awake. He wasn't sure how long he had been sleeping but had amassed a pool of saliva down the side of his cheek. He was groggy and confused as he wiped the residue away. Looking out the window he saw the roads much busier than he had seen for some time and reasoned that he must be getting close to the airport. There were four lanes of traffic heading the same direction and tall advertising boards populated each stretch of the freeway, promised all sorts of benefits and amazing offers.

Unaware at the time of choosing, Charles had inadvertently sat on a seat above the wheel and each bump in the road was now being emphasised. The heat on the bus was also unbearable; it was almost as if the elements were conspiring to punish Charles for what he was doing. He felt ill.

******

Robert awoke feeling refreshed and revitalised. The basking sunshine gave his surroundings a golden glow and as he woke he felt invigorated by the pleasant scenes around him. By now it was the mid afternoon which meant that Sophia would be back home. He stretched his muscles like a runner at the start of a marathon and headed back towards the entrance to the park.

He made the journey to Sophia's in quick time and as he rapped her door he felt nervous. The walk over had given him the opportunity to try and process a number of things in his head but now that he was standing in Sophia's doorway he wasn't sure what conclusions he had reached.

Sophia appeared at the door just as Robert was about to knock for a second time. She looked a bit tired from work but had a welcoming smile.
"Hello," replied Robert as he stepped inside and gave her a hug. Sophia could sense something was up.
"Is something the matter?"
Robert proceeded to relay the events of the previous night up until his ousting from the house this morning. After he finished he stood silent for a few moments, allowing Sophia an opportunity to process the information. He studied her expression as she duly did so and after a few seconds she astutely identified the key question that Robert had been contemplating over and over again.
"So what are you going to do now Robert?"
"I....I...I don't know Sophia. I mean, my father is convinced it's not safe to stay, and he's right about that."
Sophia looked disappointed.
"But, I don't know if I can be responsible for looking after him anymore. My life has been on hold for the past few years and now....."
He reached out and held her delicate hand in his.
"And now I think I've found something, and someone, that I want to build a future with."
A smile came across Sophia's face but it disappeared shortly after.
"Sorry Sophia, have I got this wrong?"
"No no, it's not that........"
"Well what is it then?"
"Robert, it's just, I don't want to be responsible for taking you away from what's left of your family. Besides, your father is right, it isn't safe for you here."
"It's not safe for you either," he replied before fully comprehending the implication.
"I'm sorry, I didn't......."
"It's fine, and you're right about that. But what will you do if you stay?"

She looked at him with longing in her eyes, Robert felt sure that in him she had found someone who could fill the void that had been left in her life.

"I'll speak with Jim. I'll be honest and explain what has been happening over the past few years. He will be well within his rights to cut me off from the work but if I can convince him that I've been carrying my father then maybe he will keep me on. Either way I think it's worth a shot."

"Are you sure you want to keep working here? If this is about your promise you can take it back. I won't mind."

Robert stared at her with conviction in his eyes.

"It's not about the promise Sophia. I really feel like I can make a difference here. Back home I was helping bent businessmen avoid going to jail or representing the interests of big business against smaller traders. There was nothing positive or noble about what I did. But here, here I can do something.......something meaningful. The fact that I promised doesn't feature in my thinking now, it's gone beyond that."

Sophia smiled as she pulled Robert in close.

"But I *do* have a duty; not only to you, but to Jim and all his team, especially the man from last night. I owe them and I intend to see it through, that is, if they'll let me."

"I'll speak to Jim for you. He and my father were very close so he should hear me out."

Robert's hands were around Sophia's slim waist and he pulled her close as he kissed her. Her body rose as he squeezed her tighter before eventually releasing her from his grasp.

"What about your father?"

"I know........I know," sighed Robert, dejected by the change of subject.

"He was dead set against staying, but then again he had been drinking and was shook up by the incident. I'll talk with him again when he's had a chance to sober up and cool off."

Sophia started running his fingers through Robert's dark hair,

"Well, if he does go, where will you stay?"

"I was hoping to talk to you about that."

*****

Charles had to concentrate to avoid being sick. Despite being on the freeway he was convinced this was one of the bumpiest journeys he'd ever been on. He was almost ready to give in but his resolve was steeled when he saw the shining sight of redemption in the form of Fort Worth airport. As the bus drew to a halt he leapt out of his seat and burst through the door. The temperature outside the bus was still warm but it felt like the middle of winter to Charles and he drew long breaths to recover from the uncomfortable journey. After a few minutes he realised he had left his bag onboard so he stepped back onto the vehicle and gathered his luggage. 'That's the last I'll see of you' he thought to himself as he stepped back off it.

The sleep had lessened the effects of the alcohol and with its spell wearing off Charles felt neither drunk nor sober. He just felt strange. The anger he had been carrying inside no longer felt as raw or as destructive but he remained steadfast in his conviction he was leaving. Accordingly he gathered his case and made for the airport terminal.

The building was heaving, packed full of travellers and smartly dressed businessmen; each with somewhere to go and an apparent rush to get there. Charles stood for a few moments, trying to gather himself as he took in his hectic surroundings. 'I could do with a drink' he thought but the flask was empty. Eventually he noticed the British Airways sign and headed to the desk.

An old woman was the only person ahead of him in the queue but Charles's frustration began to grow as he listened to her conversation with the assistant. The woman was arguing vehemently that she had booked a different flight but the attractive woman behind the desk continually explained that the booking had been taken as instructed. With each delivery of the same news the older woman became more and more agitated, until eventually, begrudgingly, she accepted the mistake. "Bloody useless," she scoffed as she walked off.
The woman behind the desk took a second to compose herself before calling Charles forward. She greeted him with a pleasant if well-rehearsed smile.
"How can I help you sir?"
"I'd like a ticket for the next flight to London," replied Charles, suddenly aware that he was sweating.
"No problem, I'll just have to see when the next available flight is."
She began typing on a large keyboard as Charles rapped his fingers along the desktop.
"Ummm, okay. I'm afraid we don't have anything left this evening so the first available flight will be tomorrow at 1pm."
This was an unwelcome delay for Charles and he knew it would be an opportunity for his conscience to interfere with his current plans. He did not want that to happen.
"Is there nothing sooner?"

"I'm afraid not sir," she replied with the same perfect smile.

Charles's frustration was bubbling again.

"Look, I have some very important business to attend to in England. I know you probably aren't allowed to do this but if you could find a way to squeeze me into the flight leaving this evening it would be greatly appreciated."

"I'm sorry sir but this evening's flight is completely full..."

"Can you not bump someone off it? Say that there's been a booking mistake?"

"I'm afraid that won't be possible sir."

The smile was beginning to get tiresome now as Charles's temper began to rise.

"You're afraid? You're afraid? Well I'm afraid that old woman was right, you are bloody useless."

The woman quickly dropped her pleasant expression.

"Sir I'm going to have to ask you to refrain from addressing me in that way. Now as I explained this evening's flight is full. Would you like me to book you a place on the 1pm flight tomorrow? And I must advise you that any travellers who are intoxicated or have consumed alcohol will not be permitted to board the plane."

This was the red rag Charles needed.

"Intoxicated? Listen to me you prissy bitch, I am completely sober. In fact I never drink!"

The woman was looking beyond Charles to try and catch the attention of a nearby security guard. The man duly spotted the commotion and confidently swaggered over with his arms by his side.

"Is everything alright ma'am?"

Before she had a chance to speak Charles turned to face the man.

"Yes. Everything is fine. Or it will be as soon as she books me onto the next flight back to England, out of this god forsaken place."

The woman rolled her eyes as she addressed the security guard.

"Well, as I explained to this *gentleman*, this evening's flight is full so he won't be able to travel until tomorrow."

"Look I know for a fact that..."

"You heard her sir, the flights full," said the man as he folded his arms, cutting Charles's sentence short. He looked at her for a second then turned his gaze to the guard.

"So that's the way it is, is it?"

"I don't know what you mean sir."

The woman interjected once again.

"As I said there is a 1pm flight tomorrow, I can...."

"Forget it! I won't stand for this sort of treatment so you can fucking forget about tomorrow's flight."

The security guard stepped forward.

"Sir I'm going to have to ask you to...."

"I'm going," snapped Charles, determined not to give the guard the satisfaction of kicking him out.

"Bloody useless," he snarled under his breath as he left the desk. Once again the woman took a second before re-adopting her polished smile.

Charles lugged his heavy case outside and set it down despondently. In this place where life was so prevalent he was alone, completely alone. As he baked in the evening sunshine the emotion which he had been running from all day eventually caught up with him. His mind was a melting pot of memories and as he tried to muddle them together he kept thinking about the two people in his life who were no longer there, his son and his wife. He could not take the pain anymore and, dropping to his knees, he broke into floods of uncontrollable tears. He muttered 'I'm sorry' as the pang of guilt refused to release him from its vicious grasp.

'How could I leave my son here alone?' he cursed angrily, disgusted by his behaviour. Occasionally images of a young Robert crept into his mind, proving more damning as he could see his wife's smiling face alongside them.

He crouched down and held his head in his hands for an age. His legs were weak; a result of the long journey and the bourbon and they began to shake as they filled with lactic acid. Soon Charles could take no more of this burning and was forced to rise to his feet. It was then that the sick feeling in the pit of his stomach tightened sharply, as if being choked from within. Charles knew what was coming and darted round the corner from the main entrance. As his body purged itself of the alcohol Charles wished he could only do the same with the sense of shame and disgust he felt inside.

Tears were streaming down his cheeks but these were no longer tears of sadness, rather they were caused by the painful stomach contractions that accompanied each heave. Assured that this was the last of them he took out a handkerchief and wiped his mouth. His hands were shaking and his entire body felt incredibly weak. He wiped his brow as it had started to sweat profusely. One final wretch, a final embarrassment, proved dry so Charles turned the corner to collect his bag, which remained obediently where he left it. Gathering the case quickly Charles headed to the bus stop. He still felt physically weak but he felt strangely better emotionally as the feeling of guilt began to slowly evaporate. As if to reaffirm this feeling Charles swore he would make things right with Robert. He made this vow not only to himself but also to Sarah; looking to the sky as if communicating directly with her. He realised that this was the first time he had felt able to speak with her.

As the bus approached to take him back the same painful journey he had just endured he began to feel surprisingly upbeat, as if a great weight had been lifted. 'The darkest hour is always before the dawn' he said to himself. And as the bus set off Charles felt like he might be heading towards redemption; perhaps the sun was finally about to come up.

******

Robert was nervous as he stood on the front step. He looked over his shoulder a couple of times before realising this made him look more uncomfortable so he faced dead ahead instead. After a short while Jim arrived at the door. He looked tired and his eyes did not display their usual warmth and zest for life. He silently opened the door and urged Robert inside.
"Come in. Can I get you something to drink?"
"I'm fine, thank you."
"Please, sit down."
Robert obliged and watched Jim pour himself a cup of coffee. He could recognise the pain that Jim was suffering; he'd seen it too many times before.
"What brings you here son?"
"Firstly Jim I wanted to pass on my condolences. I know that Louis meant a lot to you and to all the people here."
"He did," replied Jim feebly as a man whose spirit had just been crushed.
"That was an incredibly brave thing he did and it is something that neither I nor my father will ever be able to repay. But I want you to know that I will not forget it and, with your permission, I'd like to speak with his family."
"I don't think that's a good idea," replied Jim sternly.
Robert was taken aback slightly.
"Very well, that's your prerogative and I respect that."
"And now....."
"And now what?"

"And now is the part where you explain to me in person why you have to leave. Why you can no longer continue to work here. That's fine, I understand. This man gives his life so that you'd be safe but you don't think....."

"Jim, that's not why I came here."

"Oh really? Your father left a message just this afternoon saying he was quitting. Said he was leaving immediately and would never be back."

Robert was visibly shocked by the news Jim delivered.

"Jim, I really didn't......"

Jim sensed that this news was a shock for Robert and some of the familiar warmth return to his eyes.

"Jim I really didn't know, honestly."

"I can tell, I'm sorry to fly off the handle."

"No problem, did he say where he was going?"

"No he didn't son, but far as I know he's gone. We had someone round the house earlier. All his stuff is gone, his room is practically bare. I figured the stuff left behind wasn't needed......but now, well, I guess it's yours."

"Gone?" said Robert, more to himself than to Jim.

"Seems that way."

Robert was silent for a few seconds as he contemplated this revelation. All the times Robert could've walked out and left him to clear up his own mistakes, and now *he* was the one left behind.

"Look Jim, that doesn't really change what I came here to say. What I mean is, I'd like.....with your permission of course.....to keep working for the Voters League."

Jim remained silent as Robert drew a deep breath.

"The truth is my father...........is an alcoholic. Has been for the past few years. He drinks to ease the pain of my mother's passing. Now, I know you wanted Charles Ainsworth QC to represent your interests but the fact of the matter is that he hasn't worked in years; that Charles Ainsworth doesn't exist anymore. As soon as she got sick I was the one keeping up his legal reputation while he tried to look after her. And when she died, well, I suppose it was my job to stop his drinking from interfering as best I could."

Jim remained silent so Robert continued.

"I know I should've been honest with you from the start. But, it's not like we had a lot of options. I mean, you weren't likely to employ an alcoholic, no-one was. That's why, since we've been here, I have been the one doing the work and trying to keep him out of the way as much as possible. Again, I'm sorry for that but I assure you that I am a competent solicitor and, before my father's drinking became an issue back home, I was forging a pretty solid reputation. I'm also well versed in American law; I was an intern at Harbison & Jefferies during my exchange year from Cambridge."

Robert looked away from the table and exhaled loudly. The ball was now in Jim's court. Jim sat back to digest this information.

"To be honest Robert, I thought there was something.......not quite right......with Charles. I mean, from the perspective of a lawyer. So while what you're saying is somewhat shocking, it also explains a few things. That said, there has been a lot of good work done to date and, from what you're saying, I guess we have you to thank for that. But, if we were to keep you on there would be a few changes."

Robert's heart was pounding; rarely had he placed so much hope in an 'if'.

"Firstly, the wage will be reduced."

"That's fine," said Robert enthusiastically.

"Second, we cannot offer you any protection."

"I wouldn't feel comfortable with it anyway."

"Finally, the house is gone. We had someone over there earlier to clear it out for a family; their house was burned down last night."

"No problem."

Jim sat back and scratched his head.

"So you're telling me you're happy to work for less money, with no protection and no home?"

"Absolutely," exclaimed Robert as he sat forward.

"For the first time in a long time I feel that I can serve a purpose and I don't want to let anything get in the way of that. This place has given me a mission, a cause, and I'm fully committed to it. Thank you so much Jim, I won't let you down. I won't let Louis's family down either."

"Ok, we'll I guess that's agreed then," said Jim as a smile stretched across his sullen face.

"Can I ask, where will you stay?"

Robert had been rising to leave but sat back down.

"I'm staying with Sophia Delamaine. We've been seeing each other for some time now."

Jim's eyes scanned the ceiling as he tried to place the name. Eventually he found the information he was searching for.

"Sophia Delamaine? Why didn't you say so? I know, sorry, I knew her father very well."

"Yeah she mentioned that you and him were close."

Jim looked at him incredulously.

"But I couldn't bring that up because I didn't want this job as a favour to an old friend. I hope you can understand that."

"I suppose I do."

"It was my plan B though," said Robert with a smile creeping across his face.

Jim laughed as the pair rose from the table. Robert stretched out a hand and gave Jim a hearty handshake.

"Thanks Jim, you won't regret this. I promise."

Jim shook his hand without speaking but Robert sensed that his mood was not quite as desperate as it had been before his visit.

Chapter Fifteen

A gentle breeze blew through his blonde locks as Williams awaited the arrival of Carter. It was almost seven and the evening rush hour traffic had long since died down. Williams was sitting at the agreed spot, the bus stop on the 43 route beyond the University, he was the only person in sight.

The wind was calm and contradicted the events of the last twenty four hours. Williams knew what Carter was going to do but he tried desperately not to think about it. 'I argued the case for him' he told himself but inside he knew, if he was brutally honest, that he had failed to convince Carter. And when Carter said 'he'd think about it' Williams knew he would not see his friend again.

His fears appeared to be confirmed as Carter arrived alone. He was smoking but looked quite relaxed, not like a man who was carrying the immense emotional burden of murder across his back.

"What's up," said Williams, studying Carter for any outward signs of emotion.

"He'd flipped man. Said he was thinking bout confessing, started crying right in front of me. "

Williams knew he was lying but it was more convenient to believe the lie; it made him feel less guilty. From now on he would tell himself Errol got what he deserved because he couldn't keep his mouth shut. This wasn't on Williams.

"Ok, so what's the plan now?"

Carter finished his cigarette and threw it on the ground before responding.

"From what I hear, the old man's skipped town. In fact last we saw him he was on a bus heading toward the airport."

"Looks like they finally got the message."

"Nah, *they* didn't. The son's staying. Turns out Errol was right, he's banging that Delamaine whore. The man must never have got pussy before cause he's gonna stay here with her, even after his old man's skipped out."

"What a joke."

"Yeah, don't it make your heart bleed."

Williams pondered this information for a few seconds.

"Well, in that case, looks like we're in the clear from last night. If the old man is gone then there's no-one who could possibly ID us."

Carter shook his head.

"We don't know for a fact that the son wasn't there. Errol might not have seen him come back. You know what he was like."

Williams' heart sank. The phrase 'was like' confirmed what he had been dreading but already knew.

"So, what are you saying?"

Carter lit another cigarette and inhaled slowly.

"I'm saying, we gotta finish the job. In fact, we gotta finish two jobs. We don't know if that Delamaine bitch has got anything on us."

Williams was certain she had nothing on him since he hadn't been involved in killing her parents but he kept this thought to himself. He couldn't remember when he started letting Carter make all his decisions but he was in too deep to stop now.

"Okay, when are we doing it?"

"We'll roll tonight," said Carter coolly.

"Tonight? You sure?"

Carter hated having his authority questioned.

"Yes I'm fucking sure. We need to move as soon as we can, there's no point waiting for them to get the police involved. Are you okay with that?"

Williams nodded, like a schoolboy being told off by the headmaster.

"You still got that piece I gave you?"

"Yeah, got it safely hidden away. The ammo too."

"Bring it tonight. I don't want to be carrying a shotgun across town."

"Okay. What time and where?"

Carter lit a third cigarette.

"In the park. 11pm."

"Where in the park, it's pretty big?"

Carter turned and started walking away;

"Just be there.........I'll find you."

******

The bright lights of the city gave way to dark obscurity as Charles watched the world go by through the window. He had spent most of his day, the parts he could remember anyway, making the journey either to or from the airport but he felt it had become a day well spent. Although not tangible, he had achieved something. So as the bus drew further away from the thriving cosmopolitan of city life Charles found contentment in the thought that he was heading towards something.

The streets became increasingly familiar as the bus approached its final destination. There were three other passengers on the bus and each sat in silence, as if attending a wake. By now night had fallen and the roads were quiet. The bus arrived ahead of schedule and Charles was the first passenger to disembark, offering the driver a wholesome 'thank you' as he exited.

The air smelt strange, almost heavy. It carried a scent that conjured a mirage of memories encompassing summer barbecues, Halloweens and Guy Fawkes nights. He thought the familiar feeling might be the smell of fire but this was not so. It was more the mood that accompanies and captures these events; a sense of occasion, of forbearing.

Charles was desperate to see Robert as soon as possible and decided to get a taxi home. However, ten minutes without any traffic convinced Charles that a taxi would not be forthcoming and so he started off walking. The roads remained eerily quiet as Charles silently retraced his walk from earlier that day. His bag was heavy and it was then that Charles realised he had not eaten anything. His body began craving sustenance but Charles's spirit remained steadfast. 'Food can wait' he thought; he was determined to get home.

It was after eleven by the time Charles rounded the top of his street. His stomach was voicing its anger at not being supplied with food but it was thirst from which Charles was suffering more.

Something about the house seemed different. Charles climbed the steps and tried his key in the front door but it wouldn't open. He glanced at the number on the side of the house to make sure it was the right one. After confirming it was indeed his house Charles tried the key one more time. Again it refused to turn and Charles was taken aback as he heard a voice from the other side of the door.

"Who's there?"

"Is this number 33?" asked Charles, perplexed.

"Indeed it is, I think you must be looking for another house."

"This is *my* house."

"Afraid not, now please, leave us alone."

"Excuse me, my name is Charles Ainsworth. I live in this house. It has been provided by Jim at the Dallas County Voters League."

Charles waited to see how this news would be received. After a few seconds the front door opened and a dishevelled looking figure stood on the other side of the glass patio door.

"Sorry, did you say your name was Charles?"

"Yes I did," replied Charles, glad that his name seemed to carry some authority.

The man unlocked the patio door and stepped out onto the porch.

"Thing is sir, Jim told me this house was ours. Said the English lawyer fella had up and left and that the house was free for my family. We got no place else to go you see."

Charles was annoyed but when looking in the man's eyes he knew he'd already been through enough; his eyes looked sorrowful and he was unable to look Charles in the face.

"That's fine," replied Charles as a wave of compassion washed over him. "Could I please make use of your telephone?"

"Of course, please come in. Would you like something to drink?"

"Yes, please."

"I think there's some bour...

"Water will be fine, thanks."

******

Williams hadn't been in the park after dark for a long time. In fact the last time he was there was with Errol. They had borrowed his dad's rifle to do some target practise but it hadn't occurred to them that it would be practically impossible in the pitch black. They lit a small fire and placed empty bottles in front, elevated on a concrete block they found nearby. Williams could still see the image through the sight of the rifle; his target illuminated by fire, as if Satan was already claiming the soul about to be released. He could also remember the feeling of power when he fired the gun. Shooting and smashing the bottle was satisfying, shooting a person could not be so easy.

Williams heard a rustle in a nearby bush and gripped the pistol inside his chest pocket. The steel felt cold and comforting. His pulse began to quicken as he heard another sound. He was about to draw the gun when a stray cat darted across the pathway and into the far undergrowth. If he hadn't been aware before he now knew his nerves were on edge.

As Carter hadn't specified, Williams decided to wait at the first bench from the entrance. It was a clammy night and the sky was threatening. In the distance he could hear the sound of rolling thunder, its menacing vibrations echoing across the night sky. Rain had not arrived yet but it was coming; only a matter of time until the dusty earth was replenished by the impending downpour. Williams sat there hoping that the rain would not come until his night was over, after tonight rain would be welcome to wash everything away.

The dim red light of a cigarette was the first sign that Williams saw. As the light drew nearer he could make out the shadowy figure of Carter. He was dressed all in black and had a dangerous glint in his eye. Williams could smell drink.
"You had to choose the first fucking bench?"
"What?"
"The first bench. If there's anyone watching or following us they won't have to go too deep into the park to find us. It's wide open."
"Chill out Carter for fuck sake," said Williams, his nerves getting the better of him, "there's no-one here besides me and I came early to make sure there was no-one around, so relax."
"Don't tell me to relax. I'll relax when the job is fucking done."
"Okay then. Will we make a move?"
"No, let's wait here for a minute, let the adrenalin start flowing."
Williams couldn't believe it, Carter seemed to be thriving on the tension that he was drowning under.
"You brought it?" asked Carter as he pulled out another cigarette and lit it.
"Yeah, it's here."
"Give me it."
Williams handed over the gun without saying a word, he felt vulnerable without its deadly protection..
"Ah yes, I remember this. And that bitch should remember it too; it was pointed right at her that night."
Again, Williams said nothing. Carter smoked half way through his cigarette before throwing it down on the path;
"Right, let's fucking go."

******

The phone rang several times before someone answered. The voice was muffled, the person had obviously been woken by the call.
"Hello Jim."
"Who is this?"
"Jim, its Charles. I'm very sorry to disturb you this late."

"Uh, that's fine Charles. I'm a bit shocked to hear from you."

"I know and I'm sorry for earlier. I'd like to talk to you about that but I know now is not the time."

"Eh, yes, well....now certainly isn't the time. Where are you?"

"I'm at my house. Well, what used to be my house."

"You said you were leaving Charles, so we offered...."

"That's fine Jim. That's not why I'm calling. I'm just trying to find Robert. Do you know where he is?"

"My guess would be he's at Sophia's."

"Sophia's? Who is Sophia?"

"Sophia Delamaine. Robert told me earlier today that he had been seeing her for a while. He hasn't told you anything about this?"

"Never said a word Jim," replied Charles, embarrassed at being the last to know.

"I think he was planning on staying with her. She lives over on Montagu Street on the far side of town."

"Thanks Jim and again sorry to wake you."

"Hold on, are you going to Montagu Street now?"

"Yes, I need to see Robert. I have a few things to sort out."

"It's all the way across town Charles and there's not likely to be any buses or taxis. I tell you what, wait there and I'll come get you."

"I can't ask you to do that Jim."

"It's no problem. Besides I'd like to speak with Sophia, she's a friend of the family."

"Well, if you're sure?"

"I'm sure. I'll get dressed and be over there as soon as I can."

"Okay, see you then."

******

The cork popped loudly as Robert poured two glasses, each one overflowing as bubbles joyously exploded within. He handed a glass to Sophia and the pair raised them in celebration.

"Wait, what are we drinking to?" asked Sophia.

Robert thought for a couple of seconds;

"A toast to a new start, new beginnings and......

"To us," exclaimed Sophia as she bumped her glass with Roberts. He nodded his approval.

"To us!" exclaimed the pair as they both took a large drink.

"Is that all your stuff?"

"That's most of it, there are a few more things but Jim said he'd give me a hand with them tomorrow."

"So you've officially moved in then?"

"I'm afraid so. Why, are you starting to regret your offer?"

"Ha ha, not at all."

"There's only one thing I'm not sure about."

"Oh, what's that?"

"Where will I sleep?"

"Well now........how about I show you?" replied Sophia as she led him by the hand into the bedroom.

******

The streets were deserted as Williams and Carter silently made their trek towards Sophia's house. Williams was growing more nervous but Carter seemed focused, like a hunter stalking his prey. He was setting a fast pace and Williams had to jog occasionally to keep up with him. As they approached their destination Williams tried to steady himself by thinking about the daring things he had done, like breaking into the house and attacking the old man but this mental psyche-up was undermined by thoughts of Errol which shattered the tough mental cocoon he was trying to create.

"We'll wait here," whispered Carter, coming to a halt at the bottom of an alleyway. From this vantage point they could see Sophia's flat. It was after midnight but most of the lights were still on.

"Okay. So what for?"

Carter looked at Williams, his face was a picture of both concentration and hatred.

"To make sure our targets are inside. And to make sure we weren't followed."

Williams nodded. The adrenaline was starting to course through his veins and he wasn't enjoying the delay. He wanted to get this over with.

The pair stood in silence behind a dumpster. Occasionally Carter would step out to look back up the street. Williams knew it was unlikely anyone would be following them but Carter wouldn't take any chances, he had played the scene over in his head many times and didn't want any unexpected hitches.

The brooding night air was once again filled with the sound of thunder; the angry, booming vibrations now much louder and closer than before. To signal a final, tearful surrender the night finally succumbed to the heavy rain that had been threatening all evening. Within a matter of minutes Williams was soaked through. He said nothing as he watched Carter smoke a cigarette, oblivious to the torrential downpour. Something then caught Carter's attention and Williams turned around to follow his line of sight.
"What's that look like to you?" whispered Carter.
Williams was straining his eyes. He thought he could make out a silhouette of a person in the window but wasn't sure. After a few seconds the shadow split into two very clear silhouettes; the pair inside had been kissing.
"Looks like someone's home," said Williams.
"Fucking nigger loving bitch," replied Carter, his words seething with rage.
"We gonna move? I'm getting soaked."
Carter pulled out another cigarette and offered one to Williams, which he declined.
"When I'm ready," replied Carter, checking his gun was loaded.

******

The window wipers made a high pitch shriek as the rain began to fall heavily.
"That's been coming," said Jim, looking to the dark clouds above through the windscreen.
"Tell me about Sophia."
"I'm not sure it's my place to...
"No, I don't mean about Robert's relationship with Sophia. I just want to know about her. You mentioned her family are friends of yours?"
Jim paused for a second, allowing them to hear another outburst of thunder, barely audible over the rattling sound of the old, decrepit car.
"Well, I don't know her all that well. I was friends with her folks, we worked together. They were such lovely people."
"*Were* such lovely people? What happened?"
"Was a terrible thing happened them," said Jim, looking off into the distance, "I'm sorry but it isn't my place to tell you about it. I hope you understand."
"I understand."
"Look Jim, I want you to know something."

Jim's eyes stayed fixed on the road. He didn't want the conversation to get heavy, especially in light of his conversation with Robert earlier.

Suddenly a bolt of lightning illuminated the sky, followed a few seconds later by a roll of thunder. The rain began to fall even heavier, as if obeying this command.

"I best concentrate on driving Charles. We can talk about things tomorrow."

"Very well," replied Charles, "have we far to go?"

"Not far."

"Listen, when we arrive could I please go in on my own first. There are a few things I need to straighten out with my son."

"Of course," replied Jim, "but in that case you best get thinking about what you're gonna say. We'll be there in a few minutes."

"Believe me Jim, I've been thinking about nothing else."

******

Perhaps it was the bubbles merrily flowing in his bloodstream but as he lay in bed Robert felt good, really good. He was on his back with Sophia resting on his chest, gently caressing his chest hair between her long delicate fingers.

"I'm so glad you're staying," said Sophia softly.

Robert nodded but didn't respond. He lay in silent contemplation; no matter how hard he tried he couldn't stop this tender and relaxing moment being interrupted by thoughts about Charles.

"What's wrong Robert?"

"Nothing."

"It's okay, you can tell me."

"I'm sorry. I should be the happiest guy in the world right now. And lying here, beside you, I am happy......it's just..."

"It's him, isn't it?"

Robert exhaled loudly, "No matter what I do it seems that I can't cut him out of my life. I'm destined to carry him around with me, one way or another."

"Listen Robert, take it from me. There's nothing worse than losing the people you love, I learned that the hard way. Now I know you lost your mum but that doesn't mean you have to cut off your dad. If you want to try find him and make things right between you, that's fine. I'll be right here waiting."

"Maybe you're right."

"I know I am."

"I'll only do it if you swear you'll be here when I get back."

"I will."

"That's very kind, now come here."

Robert pulled Sophia close and kissed her.

"There's just one thing were missing."

"What's that?"

Sophia lifted her empty glass from the bedside table.

"Oh I see. Coming right up."

Robert rolled out of bed, allowing Sophia to stretch out and occupy the vacated space. He pulled on his boxer shorts and lifted the two champagne flutes before heading towards the kitchen. He set the glasses on the counter and lifted the champagne bottle; raising it to his lips to take a large swig. His hand was steady as he filled the first glass to the brim. He then started with the second but the bottle soon ran empty.

Robert held both glasses up to eye level but this comparison was interrupted by a blood-curdling scream. The voice was coursing with terror, shocking Robert into dropping the glasses and they smashed loudly on the floor. He sprinted down the hall and burst into the bedroom.

He discovered Sophia being held by a masked stranger; an arm around her neck and a hand across her mouth. She was struggling with the intruder but he was behind her and clearly much stronger. Seeing the panic in her eyes Robert charged towards the intruder but he didn't notice another person in the room. The sound of a shot pierced the air and Robert fell to the ground; an intense pain burning in his left shoulder.

"You fucking missed," said the man holding Sophia.

"No, I didn't," replied the second man coolly, "I don't want to kill him quick. I want him to see what we're gonna do to his bitch girlfriend."

Robert felt the anger flare inside him and he struggled to his feet, only to be knocked back down with a painful blow from the butt of the gun. Sophia shrieked as Robert collapsed to the floor, blood flowing from a large wound above his eye.

"This wasn't the plan man. I didn't sign up for this."

"You'll do what I tell you to do," replied Carter, pulling up his dark balaclava to release his golden locks.

As Robert lay prone on the floor he saw a flash of recognition followed by a look of terror in Sophia's expression. He turned to face the man who shot him and noticed the scar across the eye.

"Oh what's that, do you remember me? That's right honey, you've seen me before. In fact, you saw me the night I got this scar."

Sophia was kicking and writhing frantically but could not escape Williams' clutches. Carter pulled out a cigarette; revelling in the feeling of dominance. He walked over to where Robert lay and kicked him viciously in the ribs. Robert felt all the breath leave his body with each crushing blow.

"Now, here's what's going to happen. First, we're going to hold your bitch girlfriend down while I show her a real man. Then I'm going to reacquaint her with her parents, then, finally, I'm going to kill you."

Carter knelt down and grabbed Robert, forcibly propping him up onto a chair. Robert tried to resist but he was close to losing consciousness. He had lost a lot of blood and at least a couple of his ribs were broken.

"And do you know why we're doing this?"

Robert's head dipped as he slipped closer towards blacking out. Carter grabbed him by the throat and lifted his head back.

"It's happening because you wouldn't fuck off back home!"

Saliva splattered Robert's face as Carter delivered his angry tirade.

"Look at the colour of her skin, it's white, but that bitch doesn't seem to know that. It doesn't make fucking sense. There's a battle raging here and you've picked the wrong fucking side!"

Carter then turned his gaze to Sophia.

"And to the victor........ go the spoils."

With all the breath she could muster Sophia tried to scream but her cry was muffled by Williams' hand.

"Look, that's enough. Let's just get this over with," offered Williams.

"Why, we're just about to have some fun," replied Carter as he paced menacingly towards the pair. Again Sophia struggled but her energy was running out. Carter ran his hand across her cheek as tears began to fall. For a moment he was fixated upon her; the look of panic in her dark eyes drawing him in.

"Look Carter, let's stop this bullshit and...."

Carter snapped out of his trance and drew his gun, pointing it at Williams.

"Don't ever tell me what to do. I'm calling the fucking shots here!"

"Okay, I'm sorry. I'm sorry."

"That's better. Now lay that bitch down on the bed."

Sophia tensed her muscles to resist but her strength was waning as her air supply had been reduced, like an antelope being hunted by a lion. Eventually she could resist no more and Williams forced her down onto the bed, still covering her mouth with his hand. She kicked violently but Carter approached the bed and was able to hold down both her legs.

"Now you're going to see what a real man is like," he whispered.

"Here, hold this," said Carter as he handed the gun to Williams. Robert sensed his opportunity and drawing up hidden reserves of strength from deep inside he charged at the unsuspecting Williams, knocking him to the ground. The impact sent a sharp pain through Robert's ribs but it also knocked the gun out of Williams' hand. It fell to the floor as the two men did likewise and they both scrambled to recover it, grappling desperately like two dogs scrapping for a bone.

Carter was distracted by the commotion and as he looked around Sophia kicked her leg up violently, striking him between the legs. He let out a harrowing howl as he crumbled to his knees. Sophia sprang to life, drawing a deep and uninterrupted breath for the first time as she darted towards the gun. She was almost there but as she stretched out her hand she felt a sharp tug upon her leg. Williams was desperately holding her while also trying to fight off Robert. As Sophia struggled Robert sank his teeth into Williams' arm, biting down as hard as he could. Williams yelled in pain and as Robert tore some flesh off the bone he released his grasp. Sophia grabbed the gun and turned to fire it but as she did so Carter knocked her arm downwards. The resulting shot went low towards the ground, accompanied by a sickening, gurgling sound. Sophia yelled in horror but as Robert rolled away he revealed a large wound in Williams' midriff. Blood was sprouting from Williams' chest and mouth and Sophia was momentarily frozen as she watched him struggle towards his last breath. Carter showed no such hesitation and swung a vicious punch, striking her on the cheek with a blow that sent her careering to the floor. Once again the gun hit the floor but this time there would be no scramble as Carter gathered it unopposed.

"You're going to pay for that."

"Leave her alone........it's me you want," offered Robert, struggling to breathe through his shattered rib cage.

"No, no, no. We're all in this together now. Don't you see, it's an eye for an eye?" Carter walked over to Sophia and lifted her up by the hair. Her face was aching and already swollen. He then threw her forcefully onto the bed.

"Don't dare move. You can watch as I kill your boyfriend."

Sophia screamed as Carter turned and pointed the gun at the prone figure of Robert. He was helpless and exhausted, propped up against the foot of the bed near the door.

"See you in hell, nigger lover."

As Carter's finger squeezed the trigger a figure dived in front of Robert, absorbing the impact of the bullet. Carter was stunned but didn't have time to comprehend the situation as a champagne bottle smashed him over the head. He fell to the floor, revealing Jim standing behind him.

"Robert?" shrieked Sophia.

Sophia darted towards Robert but Jim grabbed her arm before she reached him. The pair stood silent as they watched Robert hold his father in his arms; tears streaming down his face. Charles had taken the bullet in the chest and Jim knew his time was running out.

"Don't give up. Stay with me, stay with me," pleaded Robert.

"Charles......Charles,"

Robert moved closer to hear his father who was struggling to speak at an audible level.

"Robert, I'm sorry I let you down......"

"You've nothing to be sorry for! Just don't go, don't leave me!"

"I've never told you this before son but...............I'm.....I've always been proud of you. You've become the man your mother and I always knew you would."

Charles's eyes rolled back in their sockets momentarily. Robert slapped his face to revive him.

"Dad, don't go."

"Robert.......please......let me go. I'll be with your mother again."

Bright red blood began spilling from Charles' mouth.

"Just remember, how proud we are of you."

With his final breath Charles's eyes glazed over and his body fell limp. Robert squeezed him but knew his father would not squeeze back. He continued holding him until he felt a hand upon his shoulder. Sophia's face was battered but her smile still made her look beautiful as she knelt down beside him. She silently held Robert as he continued to stare at his father's body. The silence was suddenly shattered by a despairing lunge from Carter, his face covered in blood. Sophia and Robert were frozen, motionless, but Carter's advance was stopped by the sound of two gun shots which dropped him to the floor. Jim nodded but said nothing as he left the room.

Epilogue

Robert's work with the Dallas County Voters League continued apace after his father's burial. He demonstrated energy and vigour that belied both his injuries and his personal loss. His determination was to create a lasting legacy following Charles's sacrifice and he successfully contributed to a series of court decisions that contributed to undermining the Jim Crow system and set the parameters for further legislative success.

The passing of the Voting Rights Act of 1965 ended legally sanctioned state barriers to voting for all federal, state and local elections.

Robert and Sophia were married on June 26th 1968; their daughter Sarah was born one year later.

Made in the USA
San Bernardino, CA
05 December 2013